TO TAME A DRAGON

DRAGON

THE PYROMAGE SERIES
S.N. MCKIBBEN

Troll River Publications

www.trollriverpub.com

To Tame a Dragon

Copyright ©2024 by S.N.McKibben

ebook ISBN: 978-1-946454-93-5
Softcover ISBN: 978-1-946454-94-2

Book Cover by: Get Covers

Editor/s: Ravi Banthia, Carol McKibben

Join the fun with Author S.N.Mckibben for giveaways, updates, and new release opportunities at: https://bit.ly/KingsThiefFree

CONTENTS

This story would not have been born had it not been for three women. Kris, Marilyn, and Patricia. For Kris telling me this had to be a longer story as a three-against-the-world theme. For Marilyn for challenging me to a dragon story. For Patricia, who constantly pushes me and said, now write it again. Preferably when not drunk.

Thank you, ladies.

I poured my soul into it.

AUTHOR'S NOTE

People don't know about the things you do for them. They won't understand the time or effort you've invested. They don't think *oh, she spent ninety minutes with me doing this thing.*

They think, "Finally, this is finished." Or, "That took a long time to get right." They disregard your time. And it's up to you and you only to say what's enough.

They will always take what you give them because they can't feel your pain, your effort, your life. They can only feel theirs.

When a person reaches beyond their own self, to look at you, to really look, they will only see themselves within you. And that's the way it should be. It should be this way because they are responsible for themselves. No other is going to know what they want. What you want.

Guard your mental health. Guard your own time. Fight for what you want. Reach for your needs. Because no one else will do these things for you. You may feel alone. But you have yourself. And that's way more than nothing.

~ S.N. McKibben

CHAPTER I

ZEROH

"INTERESTING PASTIME FOR AN assassin." The barkeep eyed the open book in my hands. He slapped a mug down on the wood-finished top, sloshing ale too close to the pages and adding another stain to the weathered cover.

My eyes rolled up to stare into the burly face of the man who owned the largest bar in the city of Aleenia.

The barkeep, whose only known name was "Barkeep," tried his best intimidation tactic by looking down his nose at me. The man could pick me up and throw me out with one arm. Not an impressive feat of strength, as I was five foot nine, and weighed no more than a nuisance. That is, if I didn't turn him to ash first.

"Listen, boy, I won't have trouble in my establishment." Barkeep picked up a rag and started wiping the inside of wet empty mugs. His forearms bulged against the rolled sleeves of his tunic while he tried pushing his too large hands inside the wide-rimmed maple tankard. Leave it to Barkeep to look intimidating doing everyday tasks.

I shook a tobacco stick out from its parchment holder, put my lips over the butt, and pulled a smoke out. The magic residing inside me warmed. As I snapped my fingers, a spark ignited. Like a wick feeding the fire, a tiny flame danced above my only unflexed digit—the middle one. I lit my tobacco stick while folding my other fingers down, expressing my thoughts on being called "boy" with a hand gesture.

"Zeroh. . ." Barkeep growled my name in warning.

The circulation in this place was horrid. I expelled smoke from my lungs. The scent of burnt parchment and dried plant-matter from my tobacco stick served to refresh the stale air. But what could I expect from a seedy tavern nestled in a remote alley of a crumbling village?

I perched the tobacco stick between two fingers, grabbed my drink, and took a gulp.

"Your establishment is safe." I threw my words at him. "At least from my fire."

If Barkeep made a scene, he'd draw attention. It was essential I didn't let my mark know I was here. Burning the alehouse down to the ground would've been my preferred method of assassination, but I liked this place too much. Not every pub in Aleenia, or any place, allowed my kind. Pyromages were dangerous, and I was on the lethal end of that spectrum.

Most mistakes cannot be undone. Some foibles can be let go with an apology. Then there are the disasters from ignorance that are unforgivable. Which was why I had to prove myself to a clan of murderers, or become a mistake of the never-coming-back variety.

Scotch burned down my throat as I returned my attention to the ancient book. A rowdy group of men cheered in the open space of the bar. They looked ready to purchase one of the rooms upstairs and have a go with one of the "available" ladies.

As long as they were away from my corner, I didn't mind. I sucked in another hit from my tobacco stick and slumped my shoulders forward to hide my face with the lapels of my coat. My head sank closer to the pages of the book.

The target was in the middle of that group of men gallivanting in the center of the tavern. Kuval was a member of a rival guild. The Acquisitions Guild employed its share of thieves called "errand boys" who gave discounts of the five-finger free variety. Merchants employed them. It kept certain businessmen operating "legitimate" shops. I portrayed a typical errand boy with my slim physique. Kuval's reputation alone could have him inducted into my guild. Arkenu's guild. Most called it the Assassins Guild. Its name alone preceded our reputation.

Kuval, my target, was the lead acquisitions agent. He was not an assassin. But when Kuval "acquired" items for his guild master, sometimes a person would be found with a knife in their body.

At first glance, a person might consider us from opposite guilds. Fortunately for me, Kuval killed in a personal way—up close, front, and center. He could afford to be that brash. The master thief had muscles that made his tribal tattoos look natural, as if he'd been born with ink etched into his skin. He used those muscles not just to steal but to kill whoever gave the Acquisitions Guild trouble. If I had to go toe to toe with someone, without magic, I'd rather take my chances with Barkeep. Kuval was honed for war while the man serving me drinks was mountainous but not dangerous.

I did better as a long-range assassin. And that's all I was good for. Some in the Aegis guild would make their targets talk, then kill them. I was no good with questions. Point at something, and it will burn. Just don't make me talk to it or care for them. The less personable meant the less I parted with my humanity. In theory. Them, they, thing, it, and that were much better on the psyche than him, he, her, and she when it came to annihilation by fire. I gave death as fast as possible. Burning had to be one of the worst ways to go, but I'd never find out. Pyromages didn't burn. Not by fire anyway.

Turning half my attention back to the tome of cursed magic, I kept the other half on Kuval. But something on the page pulled my attention. A strange dagger with a key inlaid in the pommel. It looked uncomfortable to hold. Illustrations showed sacrifices of the sharp end of this dagger imbedded inside a person and the pommel inserted into the keyhole of a door. The door to hell. The Devil's Dagger was the only thing blocking an ancient demon army. Or so the book said. And people said reading was worthless. That's why they didn't know anything of worth.

A shift in movement brought my attention back to my target. Kuval moved like a panther sliding up to higher ground before pouncing on a buckeye doe. He advanced toward me, and I did my best to blend into the wall beside me. But Kuval's presence physically reached out and sent a wave of unease through my corrupt soul.

People didn't ignore Kuval. Already, I could feel the aura of his dynasty. The man's list of deeds was longer than a palace corridor. Hell, as he strode up and loomed two feet away from me, his confidence washed away my pride, courage, and mental fortitude. The essence of vigor and charisma himself leaned so close I smelled his musk washing over me.

My hands shook, and smoke wavered its wispy tentacles in my face. I smashed the tobacco stick out in a tray on the bar. The guild master would be less than pleased if I got caught. Hell, he'd be pissed if he knew what I was doing.

Kill the mark. Raise the Assassins Guild's reputation. Make Arkenu proud for taking me in. Then maybe I'd be accepted as a full-fledged member.

The feeling of being stared at unnerved most people, especially the guilty, and it wasn't long before I glanced at Barkeep. His eyes were turned away on the person next to me. I tried to force my eyes down, but some other command told me to face the danger. I turned to glance at Kuval.

The acquisitions agent beamed at me, and his smile widened when our eyes met.

Shit.

All my concentration went to keeping my magic from blazing outward. I snapped my face back down to the book and turned pages, but I couldn't read a *fúrr* damn thing. My inner pyro hadn't threatened to rage out of control like this in a long time. But I told Barkeep I wouldn't burn down his place, and that's what I would *fúrr* damn do.

"You're, Zeroh, right?" Kuval leaned his back on the bar, resting his elbows behind him. His smiling face pointed right at me.

It was my eyes that always gave me away. I'd never found another human being with Fire burning within their pupils. Literal Fire danced in my eyes like a Hessian princess taunting the next unfortunate soul to their death. People had blue, green, or brown eyes. Flames danced where color should be in mine, as if my irises were fuel for the flames. Those that didn't know me, knew *of* me.

I responded to his query with a sideways glance and returned to "reading."

Heat rolled off Kuval's bare chest. The type of heat that crawled down my spine and made me feel like a slab of meat.

"Yeah. . ." Kuval rolled a lazy wave my way. "You're the secret weapon the Kenwald guild keeps stashed away."

My vision narrowed trying to ignore this force of nature posing as a man. The masculinity incarnate probably had no trouble with women. I was his polar opposite. His silky blue-black hair, skin that matched his mocha eyes, and strong jaw was in deep contrast to my tossed-salad white-blond mane and my complexion that never saw the sun.

"So what?" The urge to set him on fire and run grew stronger.

Kuval licked his lips. "Why don't you join us?"

My mind went utterly blank. *Join you?* "I already belong to the Kenwald guild."

He smiled like he'd won a new contract. "I meant, join our party." He waved to the group beyond the bar. "You looked like you could use some fun."

"No, thanks," I said with as much bland neutrality as I could muster.

Kuval turned his back to the bar and leaned against the top with a nonchalant air. His eyes raked me up and down. I'd just been visually molested. I wanted to leave and wash away his leering glances. Of course, my way of "washing" was burning his face off.

"You sure? You haven't stopped advertising since you walked in here." He pointed up and down at my chest.

I looked down at myself without thinking. *Advertising?* My shirt was open because, duh, Pyromage. I radiated warmth. A closed shirt would be uncomfortable. I wore the same black pants, the same unbuttoned white shirt under my open black coat every day. A show of proof I wasn't carrying a weapon. Of course, I was the weapon.

"He don't know what you mean," Barkeep said. "The boy can hardly bother to button his pants or lace his boots, much less keep the rest of himself covered. Or groomed."

I huffed at the insult and raked my fingers through my hair.

Kuval casually reached out, lifted back the side of my coat, and exposed my bare chest. I slapped his hand away and leaped back, hitting the wall. My book resounded with a *clomp* to the floor.

His eyes were fully dilated and his lips curved in a mischievous grin. Fire walked up my throat, and my magic rolled down my arms, forcing its way out in defensive maneuvers.

"Zeroh!" Barkeep's voice broke through.

Barkeep wouldn't allow patrons to brawl in his establishment. If Kuval didn't attack, I'd keep my promise. *Don't burn his pub down. You like this alehouse. Barkeep lets you drink in his tavern.*

The assassin let out an appreciative whistle. "Wow. If the eyes are windows to the soul, then you're burning inside."

I rolled my eyes. "My *soul* is about to leave you as a pile of cinders."

"Take it outside!" Barkeep leaned over, both palms on the bar top. He was ready to swing over to our side and throw us out. I scanned the pub. Everyone was watching us. Perfect. Witnesses. Not good.

I scooped up my book and hurried through the alehouse door into the dingy alleyway. Brick buildings led the dark path. Dirt, glass, and trash tumbled through the alleyway. Damn. I was going to have to make my move when Kuval was alone. In a private place. I'd been following him for two days and planned on completing my task tonight. This scene would make me suspect. But that was something to think about later. First, I had to get out of this confined lane.

Behind me, the hinges of the bar door creaked. Wood banged into brick.

"Zeroh, wait!" Kuval's voice boomed.

If I weren't out-of-my-mind terrified, I might have turned around. *No. Don't turn around. He's an honorable killer. He doesn't sink daggers in his targets back side. If I keep running...*

Arms tackled me from behind, and a heavy body pushed me down to the ground. My book went flying. I fell face-first. Then I was crushed by the weight of whoever was on top of me. Most likely Kuval. I couldn't draw breath. Couldn't scream. Couldn't talk.

"Jeez, kid. I just wanted to apologize." Kuval's lips were right next to my ear. I did not want to think about the hardness he pressed up against my ass. I tried to tell him to get off, but I couldn't speak. All the air in my lungs whooshed out when we fell. In defense, my body started warming up. My Fire rose. Small flames licked my body. *Fúrr* surrounded me, protecting me from the threat on top of me.

"I wouldn't do that." Kuval fisted my hair and slipped a blade under my throat. "If you burn me, then you'll never hear my 'I'm sorry' speech."

I calculated while his heavy body crushed my thin frail frame. Just because I couldn't burn didn't mean I couldn't be killed. It just meant he'd have to use other methods besides fire. Cutting my throat would do it. But did Kuval have enough control to slit my neck before I burnt him to a crisp?

Kuval's wave of confidence washed over me again. This man could set himself on fire and have enough control to not scream. He'd burn, but not before killing me. If that was his goal, I'd be dead already. It wasn't worth the risk. I tapered off my magic as much as it let me.

"Good choice," Kuval whispered. "Now answer me this, are you interested?"

I wheezed for air. The unease of Kuval pinning my body made me jittery. "Get. Off."

He huffed, "Damn, there's just no substance to you at all." Kuval shifted, allowing me to breathe. I gasped, trying to recover my wind.

"Did you trade physical strength for magical power or what?" Kuval said into my ear. The blade biting at my throat.

"No," I hissed. "Magic makes one lazy."

A hearty masculine laugh rumbled and echoed off the buildings of the alleyway. "Spoken like a true dragon!" Kuval said.

Dragon? Whatever.

Once he was done being amused, he turned my head. Maybe to allow me a view of his glorious face. Maybe to make me comfortable. A fat lot of good that did with my arms pinned between his thighs while he sat on top of me. But my legs were free.

"Answer me, are you interested?" Kuval dug the knife into my throat and pulled my head higher.

"Interested in what?" But in the back of my mind his intention was obvious—I just didn't want to think about it.

He eased up on my hair but not the knife. "So, you're not interested in men? That's too bad. I'm sorry then, for hitting on you. But in my defense, when a guy like you walks into a bar looking all disheveled and sexy, I notice."

"Not much of an apology," I said, stalling for time, letting my magic build. "And even if I were interested, it's shitty of you to propose a date with a knife to my throat."

"You've been following me for two days. What am I to think?"

Damn. I prided myself on being able to watch a target without actually looking at them or being noticed. But I'd managed to gain Kuval's attention. It was always my eyes.

"What gave me away?" I had to learn for next time what not to do.

"Are you kidding? I'd notice that sexy body wrapped in a burlap sack. . ."

This body, other than being on the frail side, also had extraordinary flexibility. I arched my back, reached up with my leg, and kicked him in the back of the head with the top of my boot.

Kuval grunted and pitched forward enough to let up on the knife. My insubstantial weight was an asset because it let me slip through almost anything, even from under Kuval's legs. I brought my arms up, hoisted him over my head, and got to my hands and knees.

My chest heaved from the crushing weight of a man able to fold me in half. But for him to do so, he'd have to get a hold of me. My magic rose. Fire tended my call. Screw subtly. I threw out my hand. From my palm, a fireball went flying towards the object of my ire.

Kuval jumped faster than a jack rabbit, avoiding my attack. When he landed, he stood there relaxed and unperturbed. "And when you were watching me in the bar, I knew you were there for one of two reasons."

I stood up and this time I threw a triple bomb. My hands flung out, and fireballs the size of cantaloupes rushed forward. Even if he jumped right or left, one of my bombs would smolder him. I could tell Arkenu mission accomplished.

Kuval turned, jumped onto the wall, and leaped from brick building to brick building over my projected missiles. A feat. Maybe not considering his long grasshopper legs. Kuval landed square and advanced towards me.

"I knew you had a hard-on for me one way or another." He grinned.

"Shut up!" I pointed at Kuval, and flame streamed out from my fingers.

That got Kuval to jump back, twist, and dodge. Empowered at his retreat, I ran towards him. Fire poured from my hands, charring brick walls as I charged. He leaped for the wall again, and this time, he caught the window sill of the second floor and pulled himself up. Kuval balanced his heels on the small ledge. "I just wanted to find out what kind of hard-on you had for me."

"I am not interested in you!" I pointed up and let the rage out. Fire tumbled out from my five fingers making a river of flames. An arc of fire shot upward. The brick building was getting torched, but Kuval wasn't even singed.

"Don't knock it until you try it." He jumped across to the third story of the opposite building, grinning so wide I wanted to punch out those pearly white teeth.

Fire rose from within, and soon, the flames surrounded my body. Engulfed in a shield of flame, wind started whipping around. Wind and Fire conspired, twirling lightning-bug embers up to the sky. I heated the air to an inferno and the wind increased in speed. Fire created a weather pocket only I controlled. Both elements, Wind and Fire, obeyed my demands. Inside my self-made tornado, the tunnel created enough air current to lift me skyward. My short hair whipped around, lashing my face and eyes. My body rose above the ground. Wind twirled me up. Fire shielded me. I would not miss my target.

The terrible combined forces picked up trash, parchment, broken pieces of wood, metal fragments, anything not bolted down, played within the debris in my spiral of death. Time to teach Kuval why people didn't fuck with Pyromages.

At a time when most people cowed in fear of me, Kuval just smiled and stuck out his chest like he'd won the ultimate prize. Bundling all my hate, I slammed my hands forward pushing all my magic through, aiming to wipe the satisfaction off Kuval's face.

Brick and glass shattered. Dust flew everywhere. I shielded my eyes from the blowback of grit flying in my face. In my rash anger, I'd used everything into destroying one man, not realizing I was three stories up.

Now without the support of the elements, I started falling. I was going to break open my skull from this height. There wasn't enough time to save myself.

Arms caught me in mid-flight. Kuval's strong chest heaved and merriment twinkled in his eyes. Gritting my teeth, I reached for my magic. He'd burn for touching me.

My head slammed against brick. My sight went fuzzy, and I heard a ringing in my head. Kuval's face circled around, and then got a whole lot closer.

Cold, hard metal encircled my wrists. The brain haze cleared, and I focused on my surroundings. My hands were behind my back, caught in iron cuffs. Kuval leaned in close and twirled a stray lock of my short white hair.

"Get off me!" I raged.

Fury balled in a compressed mass, hovering within my solar plexus. A wall of flame surrounded me like an aura. Kuval jumped back. Without my hands free, I couldn't direct my Fire, but I could use it to defend myself from perverts that didn't understand the meaning of "no."

Kuval pulled out a metal rod with a clamp at the end. He flicked the device and the rod extended. The clamp closed around my neck. I pushed against the restraint. The muscles in Kuval's shoulders and forearms bulged as he worked at pushing me back. In truth, his effort was more than a match for me. I wouldn't win in a contest of strength against him. He shoved me against the wall, and I sank into a defeated slump.

The compressed magic in my chest expanded in a last effort to win. A wall of Fire grew outward. It extended in a wild bubble of plasma, but my range did not reach the end of Kuval's metal contraption. He gritted his teeth, and his arms started shaking. His right foot pushed against the wall behind him while the other foot steadied his leaning stance. Beads of sweat drifted down his tattooed arms and chest. His half-naked body became slick. The heat was getting to him. Like any other human, my Fire would melt his skin off if he was too close.

A spark of hope ignited within, and I stood with renewed will. I stared down into his determined face. Kuval pushed me against the wall. His knuckles darkened. His bold smile faded, and Kuval's face shaded with a grim fortitude of a man who lived for something. His stare pierced into my soul. He possessed the strength of a tiger and the will of a phoenix. That's when I knew. He'd be charred black, and Kuval still wouldn't give up.

"We could be really good together." His face crumpled into a cruel mask—the mask of an assassin who had no choice.

I flinched, shoving out thoughts of what he implied by "together." Kuval yanked the rod. With my neck encased in the ring, I had no choice but to fly forward. He shoved me back. My skull hit the wall.

"Stop or I'm going to bash your head in."

He'd made his point. With my hands and head controlled, there wasn't much I could do. If I didn't stop, he'd bash my brains in. In my predicament, he could easily kill me. He wanted information. There was a slim chance I could talk my way out of this.

I closed my eyes and settled the magic rolling in chaos through my body. I calmed the emotions fueling my flame. The raging torrent died to a dirt devil, then a breeze, and finally a soft glow letting the element settle to a flicker within my lungs.

Kuval grunted. His hands were a mess of blistered flesh, but he still clung to the metal pole. He'd withstood more than I'd thought. Kuval pushed a button on the end of his pole and the rod extended out behind him. The butt end dug into the opposite wall, pinning me to the building at my back. Anyone wanting to go down the corridor would have to play limbo. But there wasn't anyone coming to save me.

My head couldn't move, my hands were behind me, and my coat was pulled back, exposing my chest for any passer-by to stick in a knife. Not that there was any traffic this time of night. Everyone kept to themselves around here. Mostly. My only satisfaction was watching Kuval sneer in pain pulling his other palm away. He gingerly pulled a canteen from his belt and washed his hands, hissing the entire time, "Damn it."

A blue vial came out of his pouch after he clipped the canteen back on his belt. Pain killer. He downed the liquid like a tequila shot. He glanced at me and squinted. "Go ahead. Keep your smugness long as you can. I've got plans for you, my friend."

"So, no quick and painless death for me."

He didn't reply. Instead, he pulled a roll out from one of his pouches and started wrapping his hands with thin strips of cloth. When he was done, he gingerly picked up my book that, miraculously, hadn't burned. Again. This was the second time it had been under fire and hadn't burned. But the book was the least of my concerns right now.

Kuval tucked the tome in one hand and took hold of the pole with the other. He retracted the end, making the staff nine feet in length instead of twelve.

"Let's go talk," Kuval said giving me a nod.

CHAPTER 2

ELDYN

"THE AUDACITY OF THAT man," I huffed and stared at the bejeweled knife inside its plush velvet case wondering an infinity of questions. *That man*, being Kuval, would be the only one in my guild that would dare return with such a dangerous magical item.

Thank goodness, I was in my office adjacent from my shop's floor. If we were out near the glass cabinets or the bookshelves, anyone could have walked in and seen this artifact. Knowing about it could threaten anyone's life, and I would not wish this object's destiny on my clients.

The *Devil's Dagger* was a unique dirk. Not long enough to be a sword, but too big to be just a knife. The blade spanned three feet in length and one inch in width, bulging near the end like a snake's throat after eating a mouse. The pommel was shaped in the form of an elaborate key.

Good.

It meant the knife was dormant. If the pommel were in the shape of a dragon head, all would be lost.

Most thought this dirk an heirloom representing power, wealth, and legend. Only the "lost son" could awaken the blade, or so that was rumored. Still, this was not a throwing knife. It was a relic thought lost in Casflamir's War. No one had seen this since Yair, the greatest of all Pyragons. Probably the greatest of *all* dragons.

As I stood in my shop with my jaw hanging open, a movement caught my eye.

Thomas, my assistant, shuffled from foot to foot, staring at the case, waiting for my evaluation. He'd come to me two years ago wanting a better life for him and his family. Knowing I was the guild master of Acquisitions, he offered himself up as a willing assistant that asked the right questions and knew when not to push. From me, he learned about relics, magic, and how to run a business.

We couldn't be more physically opposite. He was tall enough to reach the top shelf that reached to the shops ceiling, while I had to look up at everyone except most women and children. His balding head contrasted my long blue-white tresses. His round face to my narrow and high cheekbones spared no similarity. His brown eyes the opposite my sea blue orbs. But we matched well in business. I was the master. He was the novice. Thomas trained hard to learn. Within two years, he learned how to run this shop of mishmash books, relics, and magic items without me for a few months. Long enough for my treks to Ekinphrow—the island only known to drakes and home to two dragons.

"Thomas?" Comfortable enough in the privacy of my office, I pulled the dagger out of its case.

The skeleton key handle wasn't made for holding but was an indication to the dagger's origins. My dragon's blood sang with knowledge of the item. This was the original box. Impossible. "Did Kuval say anything about this? Like, where he got it?" Or why he gave it to me? Did he know what it was? If so, was he offering me, a drake, the honor only a dragon should have?

No. I shook my head to myself. Knowing Kuval, he'd arm wrestled this artifact from someone, knew that it was useless for throwing or fighting, wasn't privy to what it was, and hoped to impress me or pawn it for some other magical item. Honestly, I didn't want to know how he got it, from who, or from where. But it was curious how he'd gotten *this* in his possession.

My bald, stout gentleman of an assistant wrung his hands and gave me a meaningful raised eyebrow. "He only told me his *price*, Master Eldyn."

I coughed and nearly choked. Kuval's price usually included sexual favors. "Of course. I assume his usual asking." Kuval had no clue as to what he'd brought me. "Did he say where he got it? No, wait. . ." I held up my sleeved hand. "Don't tell me. I don't want to know." Knowing who the original owner was would certainly bring trouble.

Thomas chuckled. "He didn't say."

"Thank mercy." These types of treasures always held a curse.

"He said he'd be back tonight. After closing." Thomas gave me a knowing smirk.

"Seriously?" I was not a revolving door. I'd gotten our relationship down to a professional basis, or at least I'd thought I'd made myself clear. I wanted to concentrate on finding *my* dragon. Kuval was only a distraction. I wanted nothing more to do with him other than business. He fetched profit but his sensual hands had gotten me into bed more times than I wanted to admit.

"So, what is it?" Thomas asked.

I flashed my best teaching smile, set the box on my desk, and held the Devil's Dagger like an auctioneer. "Use your knowledge and hazard a guess."

Thomas scratched his head, eyeing the gemstones on the hilt and casting a gaze over the blade. "It looks like a statement piece. Something a noble would commission." But he grimaced and squinted at the handle. He knew on instinct what was wrong. Thomas tended to state the least likely possibility first.

"Or?" I prompted.

"The jewels are worth something, so maybe it's for some ritual?"

"Very good," I beamed. He wouldn't know about the Devil's Dagger because it was dragon lore. But that didn't stop him from using logic to figure out the value of an item.

The outer bell rang. We had a customer.

Thomas raised both bushy eyebrows. "Are we still open?"

I rolled my eyes. "Might be *himself*." Despite my self-righteous pep talk, my stomach fluttered at the thought of seeing Kuval.

My assistant left me to my new acquisition. This relic was too powerful in the wrong hands. There was something off about all this. If the blade surfaced after a three-hundred-year hiatus, it meant big things were happening. Not just in Aleenia, but in all of Neith.

It could also mean my dragon might finally surface. The one in my dreams, calling to me. The one promised to me by the Veteris.

A presence invaded my physical space, as if an invisible pair of eyes was on me. Not good. I started to walk toward the back of the office where a door separated the buildings living quarters from the business half. I could hide the dirk in my bedroom. No, the kitchen. Wait. This thing couldn't cut fruit. It would be too out of place there. The living room? Too obvious. No, I had to keep this with me. Anyplace else would be a liability. I whispered a prayer of forgiveness to the Devil's Dagger for my rough treatment and stuffed the knife inside the spelled pocket of my robe.

Thomas rushed into my office, nervous and shaking.

My heart jumped from my chest to see my assistant so rattled. "Thomas?"

"The Aegis. . . Arkenu. . ."

"Kenwald?" My chest thudded.

He nodded.

"Such *perfect* timing," I uttered.

A relic and now the Assassins Guild Master. There are no coincidences. I smoothed over my blue-white locks and made sure my diamond teardrop-shaped earrings faced bottom down. Recalling happy thoughts brought a natural smile to my lips despite the possibly deadly conversation ahead.

I stepped out of my office and into the showroom.

There stood the commanding, cloaked figure of the master of assassins. Arkenu was incognito. Not a good sign. He was a man who preferred to take matters into his own hands. Especially for high-end "situations." His motto, *justice by my own hand*, proved fatal to those who crossed him.

I dipped my head in respect, treating Arkenu with as much deference as a noble. He was as dangerous as a venomous snake. *Show no fear.* "What may I do for you, Master Aegis?"

His sly glance measured me up and down. Sexy *and* dangerous.

"Eldyn, you are rather important here in Aleenia."

Threatening me already? I hoped he was only after the Aegis guild *security tax*. "I only do what I can."

"I've made it safe for you here for a long time." His *for free* was implied, but nothing was ever free. Security tax only went so far when one was a drake. If humans found out my genealogy, well, it would be bad.

"I do appreciate you." *So, just tell me what you want and be done with it.*

"I give my services to you because of your stature."

"Yesss. . ." I hissed air. *Please don't draw this out like a nihilistic regent.*

"Eldyn, this is important." Arkenu peered out from under his hood. A serious face for a serious man. At least, he did not take his occupation lightly.

"Arkenu, I am aware of your security." *That also poses as spies.* "I understand the effort you maintain on my behalf as unnecessary as it is."

"Is it unnecessary?"

My smile fell. "Is there a pledge out for me?" Was he warning me? Had I pissed someone off? Did they know what I was?

"Not yet."

"Don't rattle me." I sighed. "Out with it."

Arkenu paused. His eyes weighing me. Assessing.

Perhaps, he wanted me to approach him. I smoothed my hands down to my sides. "Customers know I am discreet. Requests are made in confidence."

"Are they?" He took a step and loomed over me.

Having had enough of the word game, I waited out his entertainment in silence.

Arkenu turned and stepped over to the glass case, examining the items.

He wanted something. Not money. But some*thing*. Of course, not believing in coincidences, I had a suspicion as to what particular item he wanted. But I wasn't going to hand the Devil's Dagger over to him. He probably knew that. Hence, this wordless mind torture. If he was waiting for me to crack, he'd be disappointed. Unbeknownst to him, drakes had a different sense of time than humans.

"Traveling merchants are those who are in search themselves." Arkenu remained focused on a bobble inside the case.

What was he getting at? "I've been here for twenty years. I don't qualify as a traveler."

"Not much for roaming?"

I shook my head. "No."

"But you weren't always." Arkenu turned towards me. "Were you?"

I pressed my lips together. Knowledge. If he went that far into my past, he might be looking for information. "In my youth, I did gallivant a bit."

Arkenu smiled.

Damnable. He'd been cold reading me, and I'd given a piece of information away. Valuable information.

Humans tended to be. . . cautious around drakes. Of course, to them I looked as if I were as old as one of their children coming of age. To my own people, I was Eldyn—elder, old, wise, ancient. But only one person in Aleenia knew I was not human. Kuval kept my secrets knowing if he didn't, it could be my death.

"Are you looking for a youth potion?" I teased the guild master.

He chuffed.

Yeah, I didn't think so either. Attempting to throw the Prince of Secrets off my path was like trying to drag a scent hound off a blood trail.

"Eldyn, I fear for your safety."

A less experienced assassin would have attempted intimidation by playing with a knife or some other deadly contraption. For Arkenu, words were his weapon of choice. His voice delivered emotional blows. He was not an amateur making overt glances at a dangerous colleague. His six-foot-two stance achieved the right amount of *leer* needed for scare tactics. The hood covering his face, leaving his expressions to the imagination, left enough of a foreboding image.

"And why would that be, Guild Master Aegis?"

Arkenu leaned closer. "People are often. . . rude when they find out people they trust are not who they claim to be." His knowing glint tipped me off to his double threat.

He would not endanger his men to murder the likes of a drake like me. All he had to do was tip people off, and my customers would kill me for him. Even Thomas didn't know I was fifty-one percent dragon. For a reason.

Ever since Casflamir's War, humans did not like drakes, dragons, or magic. Though they didn't mind partaking in the later.

Arkenu's ability to wield justice and get "the people" on his side was bar none. Even though I could defend myself from an angry mob, I would still suffer. Who among Aleenia would support my boutique after knowing I was a drake?

I shrugged. "Many would gossip, but without proof. . ."

Arkenu leaned forward, showing me as much of his chiseled face as his hood would allow. Eyes black as coal glimmering with the malice of a hardened war chief. "You are no fool."

The master assassin tired of this game. He stayed silent and let me stew my own fabrications of consequence. I could imagine my store burnt to the ground. The people I cared for dead. My own life in jeopardy.

Footsteps scuffled behind me. Thomas.

The guild master rose to his full height and pulled back his hood, revealing a cunning smile to my assistant. "Good man. Thomas, is it?"

"Yes." Bless my helper who stood firm but with a drawn, pale face.

"Has anything of interest been admitted lately?" Arkenu kept a friendly, amenable voice. Which made him all the more terrifying.

Thomas turned his attention to me. I smiled brighter than usual. *Please, Thomas, tread with caution.*

"I can't say." Thomas wrung his hands and flashed a nervous smile.

"Can't usually means won't." Arkenu stalled for a moment, then stepped forward.

I grabbed the guild master's arm. "Don't."

He halted and turned his eyes to me. "Give it to me."

The corners of my lips quirked up. Just as I was going to give a facetious answer, Arkenu slammed me to the wall. His hand covered my throat. My vision faded. I couldn't breathe. My reaction was instinctual. I called upon Vesi and pulled forth the water within Arkenu. Liquid streamed from the corners of his eyes.

"Let him go!" Thomas cried.

"Stop," Arkenu growled, his eyes two burning coals.

I grabbed his arm and squeezed. In a rasp, I spoke, "Let go."

He pulled back, letting me breathe. The force of the choke made me wheeze and sputter.

"Master!" Thomas came running. I pushed my second behind me and stood in battle stance.

Arkenu recovered quickly and raised a hand in supplication. "My apologies. I am impatient. The last piece of the puzzle has come into play."

"If I say we don't have new stuff. . ." Thomas wielded his anger toward the guild master of Kenwald.

"Thomas. . ." I shushed my assistant with a pat on his arm.

The assassin straightened and cast a sweeping hand to my assistant. "Isn't he your apprentice? Won't you tell him what he's willing to die for?"

Thomas's complexion went gray. "Die?"

My assistant was not yet adept at translating an assassin's language. I'd never wanted this for him. He had a home. Family. A daughter. A wife. A profession. Happiness. I would not let Thomas get involved in any of this.

Arkenu turned his attention to my assistant. "Since your teacher is resistant, I can enlighten you."

"Don't." I clenched my teeth.

"The Devil's Dagger is not just any knife."

"All right!" I raised my palm to stop Arkenu's speech.

"Master?" Thomas's eyes held a desire to understand. A quality I admired while instructing him, but very bad in a situation like this.

Turning to my assistant, I lowered my voice. "Remember what I've told you about knowledge?"

He nodded. "Knowledge is power."

"Do you remember the rest of it?" *Everyone forgets there is a balance in all things.*

"Yes, master."

"Repeat it."

"Knowledge is a double-edged sword. It can give you power, but if you don't have the means to protect it, that knowledge can kill you."

Good. He remembered. I lowered my voice for only him to hear. "If you know, you're a witness. What happens to witnesses here?"

Thomas's eyes widened. He understood. Witnesses disappeared. One never revealed what one knew. Not unless necessary or for profit. But only when that knowledge wouldn't come back and take a chunk out of the knowledgee's ass. If I hadn't known about the Devil's Dagger, I might happily have handed it over to Arkenu. But if that happened, if I gave the talisman to the assassin, a human. . . no.

"It would be in the right hands." Arkenu stepped forward.

I whipped around. "Don't move."

He took me seriously and halted. "Eldyn. . . Elder. Wise one. Ancient Water Weilder. . ."

My heart sank. There was no mystery if Arkenu knew I was a drake.

Arkenu continued, "I implore you to think this through. Desperate men take unfathomable risks. Do unfathomable atrocities. Prejudices make men do things even worse in the name of righteous condemnation. They turn on friends, lovers, their own blood."

His bread crumbs of information left just enough to expose me to those who understood about drakes but left the unlearned ignorant. Thank all that Thomas was not wise to the ways of drakes.

"I know you have it." Arkenu held out his hand.

"Spies are good for that." I narrowed my eyes at the Aegis.

"No. I know." He pressed his palm over his heart.

"You are not the forgotten prince," I snarled.

"How can you be sure? Prophecy says. . ."

"Prophecies are wrong!" Oh, how I knew prophecies were shit drippings.

Arkenu leaned back and eyed me. "All the same." He held out his hand.

I pushed Thomas backward, towards the door. This megalomaniac thought he was the descendant of Yair. No. It didn't work that way. He was pure human. Not even one percent dragon. I couldn't be paid to consider the notion. Prophecy be damned.

"Perhaps, you're not as smart as I thought." Arkenu dropped his arm.

He wasn't going to chase after us. That meant he either had a man by the door or was confident he'd catch up.

Maybe both. Scenarios played in my mind. All of them left Thomas dead. Unacceptable.

"If you're thinking your Acquisitions friend can help you. . ." He waved a hand in the air, as if he were sweeping away all obstacles. He did not finish his sentence and let my thoughts make their own conclusions.

"Kuval?" I smiled understanding Arkenu made light of the one person he could not best in an attempt to diminish Kuval's significance. "He can take care of himself."

"True, he does *play* at challenging rogue dragons, but I wonder how well he does against one that is trained to kill."

"I'm sure he's fine." I'd heard rumors of a Pyromage inside the Kenwald guild. Didn't mean he was a dragon. He could be a drake. Arkenu was trying to bait me.

"Then you haven't heard? I'm surprised, Eldyn. Mayhap, you're losing your touch."

I clenched my teeth. He was pushing all my buttons. "Rumors tend to grow egos. A Pyromage does not a dragon make."

"Ah, so you have heard of our newest member."

This conversation was getting too risky—for Thomas. The more he heard, the more he'd understand. The more in danger he'd be. "Thom. . ." I whispered over my shoulder. "Your duty for the day is done. Go home."

"Hazardous decision, isn't it?" Arkenu stood without a care in the world. "You'll be left alone."

"Thomas?" I looked back at my assistant.

His wide eyes were glued to Arkenu. He was terrified. "I'm not leaving you."

"Leave, or I'll terminate your employ."

"Then I guess I'll look for a job tomorrow."

I could only hope he'd feel the same way if he knew I was a drake. Probably not. "Thomas," I growled.

He grabbed my wrist and started for the door.

Arkenu waved a hand at my shops front door. "Try your luck, intern."

"Thomas, stop. He has men posted outside." I pulled Thomas back the best a cat could stop a river horse.

The guild master held out his hand. "Give me the dagger."

"No," I snarled.

A genuine smile crossed Arkenu's face. "Since you have been generous in your confession, I'll offer a trade."

Childish bastard. "I won't hand it to you."

"Then don't."

I narrowed my eyes. What was he playing?

"Trade. Your assistant's life for you."

"Just me?" I asked.

"No," Thomas said.

"Just as you are." He smiled at me.

A promise from Arkenu was as good as a bank note in hand. Arkenu's negotiation skills were legendary. He didn't use force or violence unless absolutely necessary. This was a man that convinced a paranoid king that his kingdom was best left in his hands. He was also unpredictable. No one knew his motives. Arkenu proved cunning and intelligent. Which meant he knew that killing me meant he would never find the dagger.

"Done." I agreed to his terms and pushed Thomas outside.

"Master!"

"Go home, Thomas." I scanned the outside for threats.

"Yes, intern." The Aegis waved his hand. "Please go now."

"Master Eldyn?" Thomas pulled at the hem of my robe.

I refused to look at him. "Get out of my sight."

"And do come back tomorrow. Make it look like business as usual." Arkenu threw a glance to my assistant. "Tell no one of our conversation. Don't worry about being short one master artisan. I'll make sure you have a man to. . . help during business hours." His pause completely deliberate.

Nice. I couldn't help but curl my lip into a contemptuous snarl. "Hurt him in any way, and you won't have air to breathe."

Arkenu lifted an eyebrow. "I keep my word."

"That's rich, coming from you." He was known to keep his word, but he was also an assassin.

The guild master said nothing. Arkenu stared me down. In the background a cloaked shadow leaned against my building. I recognized him as Arkenu's right-hand thug. Bemus.

"I don't like this." My assistant refused to go. He still clung to my sleeve. "What do I say to the other guild members?"

"Damnable, Thomas, my life is in your hands. Don't tell anyone about this. Leave now. Come back tomorrow. You can run the shop on your own." My shortness almost brought the man to tears.

Thomas dropped my sleeve and looked around. I was sure he saw what I knew. Where Arkenu went, the rest of the Kenwald guild wasn't far.

"You're a strong man," I said to my assistant. "But you can't take them all." And if *I* did, he might get hurt in the process.

Finally, resignation filled his eyes, and he looked to Arkenu. "What will happen to him?"

"I will not hurt him, noble Thomas. I will feed him and house him until he gives me what I want." Arkenu slapped a hand on my shoulder.

I refrained from wincing.

Thomas turned to me. "Why not give it to him?"

Closing my eyes, I willed him to understand. *The Devil's Dagger was not something you hand to anyone.* If he'd caught the name of the artifact, he might leaf through my tomes and find out why.

"All right then," Thomas said. "I'll be back tomorrow."

I let out a breath as Thomas walked east towards his home, and we waited until his shadow crested over the horizon.

Arkenu closed the shop's front door and gave a bird call.

"I should lock it." Maybe I could get back inside, distract him, and get away. "I left my keys. . ."

"Your shop and your wares will be fine." Arkenu leveled his gaze as if to say, *I'm not stupid.*

Well, it was worth a try. I followed the guild master out. We walked northeast, towards Brogan Prison just as the sun dipped beyond the sea.

CHAPTER 3

ZEROH

Kuval's self-satisfied smile irked me. Mostly because it seemed like a genuine smile. He was the only person that probably didn't have a care in the world. Even while fighting. Even with that look of determination stripping my insides. His face held conviction and a life-knowing affirmation.

Only those that knocked on the gate of hell, begging to be let in, begging for release from life, were my kin. Confidence, faith, sentiment—none of these words described me. But Kuval sweated out such creed without his notice.

He took the pole-clamp contraption and hoisted the rod over his shoulder lifting me into the air by my neck. My head ached like it would detach from my body. In an instant, I was choking, gasping for breath, kicking my legs, and trying to free my arms.

"Oh, sorry." Kuval glanced back with an evil twinkle in his eye. He leaned the pole down just enough so I could tiptoe my way down the alley. I could barely breathe. This clamp-rod was an effective method of transporting a prisoner—me—from point to holding cell.

As we walked, Kuval took side streets and dark lanes through the city. Few candles offered light on our way. Those glancing out their windows didn't linger, especially those that met my eyes. The sparse people we did pass didn't give me a second glance. We were in Kuval's territory. These people were not of the upscale variety. Their clothes were cloaks, rags, or nonexistent. I didn't expect any of them to go out of their way for me. Not for a Pyromage. None spoke, and few glanced at my predicament. There wasn't a curious eye among them. These were the hopeless, the broken, and the forgotten masses of Aleenia.

Crumpled multistoried buildings eclipsed the moonlight as Kuval strode down the dirty streets. Most buildings were made of brick and mortar. Others were shack-like, made of wood. All of them were run-down, poorly made, or on the verge of collapsing. The wretched underbelly of Aleenia was a good place to hide, or sequester a Pyromage.

Kuval jostled me around like a successful hunter bringing dinner home to his family. "This place used to be the jewel of Neith."

All I could answer was a grunt. Though I wasn't really answering him. More like trying not to suffocate as we walked.

"But that was back when Yair ruled."

"Yair is a myth," I spouted.

He washed a *what-do-you-know* eye over me and kept his steady pace.

The Brogan Prison came into view. Shit. Was he turning me in? Arkenu had forbidden us from attacking Kuval; maybe the thief knew that. I would flame out, and ash a crap-load of guards before going in there like this. It housed the worst of the murderers, thieves, and unsanctioned assassins. Its surrounding wall was fifteen feet high. The prison itself was a four-story mass of thick stone. Brogan Prison was also my home. Or rather Arkenu's home base, so I stayed there as did all my guild mates. Going in with my feet dangling would make Bemus howl in laughter, and my guild master might decide I wasn't worth the effort anymore.

"They'll arrest you," I said.

Kuval looked back at me again. All he gave me was his confident smile. Great. Humiliation seemed headed my way.

But he turned away from the prison and headed into downtown. As he walked and I choked, tiptoeing down the cobblestone, the moon cast its last light before hiding behind the western mountains. The tin roof of the water tower that supplied the eastern part of the city reflected the moonlight. The tower became bigger as we got closer. Finally, as buildings dropped off into grass fields, it was apparent that the water tower was where we were headed.

Smart. Water combated Fire with vengence and tenacity. A Pyromage was weakest around Water. Kuval knew his stuff.

When he turned down a flight of cracked stone steps, it was the first time my heels touched the ground, and I could truly breathe. Darkness enveloped Kuval as he stepped into an alcove. Metal keys jingled, and a door creaked open.

"Don't flame up, or it will become very wet for you all of a sudden."

My neck got jerked forward, and I went down into the darkness. Stairs led to a very large, dark room. Cold stone assaulted me with its musty mold-ridden ambiance. My insides began crackling against the element of Water floating in the air. I shielded myself with the thinnest layer of heat to dry out my surroundings.

The place was equipped with a knee-high stone altar equipped with clamps at each corner. It reminded me of a sacrificial table.

A pipe system ran along a wood ceiling. If my hands were free, I could reach up and touch the panels. Kuval's height was nearly too much for the short ceiling. We were directly under the water tower.

"Word of caution," Kuval said. "I don't know how much water there is above us, but it's enough to last all of Aleenia for three days."

"So. . . *don't* burn the ceiling."

"I'd be fine." He spun the key ring on a finger. "You, not so much."

"Perfect place to sequester a Pyromage." Fire and Water did not get along. I didn't have a problem drinking ale, lemonade, anything that muddled pure water. Dehydration affected even me. But since I carried the element of Fire, fresh Water did not treat me kindly.

We walked inside, and my sight adjusted. Jars, beakers, and other equipment suited for a madman's laboratory sat on a long wooden table spanning one side of the room. Along the wall was a small kitchen, if one called a sink and a butcher block a kitchen. Otherwise the room seemed sparse.

Once inside, Kuval turned me around and walked me backward until the back of my knees hit solid rock. He'd backed me up to the altar. I had no choice but to sit down. He appraised me turning the clamp-pole side to side, forcing me to twist back and forth.

"I'm guessing you'd rather see it coming." His eyes sparkled with mirth.

Oh shit. He was going to kill me. "No—"

He pushed the rod, choking me as I slid up the altar. Kuval stepped up, hovering over me with his feet straddling my hips, and shoved me on my back. My arms and hands didn't have anywhere to go since they were locked behind me at the small of my back. My open coat fell away exposing my pale, hairless chest. Kuval gave me an appreciative look and spread my legs out, using his feet, kicking my ankles into the altars clamps and locked my legs so they couldn't move.

"Do you know what the other name for the Acquisitions Guild is?" Kuval eyed my body.

"Vandfald."

"Very good. Do you know what vandfald means?" He held onto the rod as a pole and swung around, enclosing my head between his boots. His hands had to be killing him, and still the buttons on his pants strained hiding the load behind their folds. If he were any more excited, they might pop.

"It means waterfall." I wanted to tell him what to do with his sizable erection.

"Again, very good." He gazed down into my eyes.

Bastard. It was obvious what he was doing. Lining up his cock and my mouth, imagining. . . I shuddered.

He released my neck from his contraption and jumped down. My legs were spread and clamped to the stone and my hands were tied behind my back. I could sit up, but nothing more.

Kuval rummaged underneath the long table. He grabbed a bucket, dipped it in a water trough, and threw liquid at me. Ice water splashed over my body.

"Motherfucker!" Water stung like a thousand paper cuts. An entire bee hive stinging me would still be better than Water searing my skin. I gasped and struggled while steam rose from my body.

"That should keep me safe for a bit." Kuval unlocked my ankles, grabbed my boots, and slipped them off. Considering I never tied the laces, it made taking them off easier. While I was still recovering from the dowsing, Kuval grabbed the top of my pants and pulled the buttons open.

"Hey! What are you doing! Get off me!" I twisted in pain and anger.

Kuval grabbed my pants and slipped them down in one swift motion as if he'd done it a thousand times. "No underwear, nice. Good thing I didn't know at Barkeep's, or I might have shoved you down on the counter right then."

I flailed my pale leg now that they were free, trying to knee him. He was gone one moment, and then another wave of ice water covered my body. This time making contact with bare skin. I screamed and bucked in pain. My body was being cut with invisible knives. Everywhere the water touched drove my Fire magic further and further into the safety of its host—me.

"Do you know why we're called Vandfald?"

"Because you're assholes," I sputtered.

He smirked. "We call ourselves Vandfald because we know how to deal with Pyromages, or in your case, Pyragons. I'm not gifted with elemental water magic, but I've got all the tricks down."

"Pyragons?" I sputtered, trying to get past the pain. If I did, I was going to rip out his throat.

"Fire dragon. Pyro dragon. Pyragon."

There was that word again. *Dragon.*

Two more buckets dowsed the fire just under my skin. My screams echoed in the stone-and-wood chamber. Kuval knew how to deal with a Pyromage, or whatever he thought I was. Throwing freezing cold water on my body would exhaust my magic. Emotion was its oxygen. Body fat was its fuel. Mixed together, I controlled elemental Fire. Most of my funds went to eating, and I was already thin. But this assault on my body would force my magic inward. My Fire would consume more body fat. When I ran out, well, it was the same when a wood fire ran out of fuel. The fire died. Since Fire was part of me and I a part of Fire—I didn't want to think about the consequences.

What Kuval was doing would make my element go to the only place that could sustain itself. Deep within me. In normal conditions, this wouldn't affect me. Give me food and drink, and it wouldn't be a problem. But I was a prisoner. Kuval would probably give me his version of a guest's welcome. That in its own way frightened me.

Already my Fire simmered in my lungs, which was fine. Fire inside or outside my body didn't hurt me. But if Kuval drowned me, put my head under water—the pain would tear at my lungs. If I couldn't breathe, neither could my magic. I'd die if the last embers of my element were snuffed out. If I remained as one of the poor souls remaining alive without Fire, I'd wish I were dead. But there was another problem. The water Kuval hit me with wasn't just water, it was elemental Water. Normal water by itself stung and hurt like a motherfucker. Elemental Water was in a league all its own. Its hatred for Fire would force its way through me, any way it could. As it was doing now.

After the fight in the alley, being choked all the way here, and finally forcing my Fire to feed off my reserves, I was exhausted. I couldn't even call flame to my fingers. Not that it would come out until I dried off.

Kuval tugged at my wet coat and shirt. "Let's take this off."

"No!" I squirmed.

He pulled away with his hands up. "I can leave it on. Whatever. But taking it off would let you dry faster."

He was right. Pin pricks stabbed tiny needles along my back. My clothes would only serve to torture me. But getting completely naked with Kuval in the room was even worse. Between painful stinging and have Kuval groping me, I chose to keep my clothes on.

I heard a squeak and running water. Above my head I saw a contraption made of bamboo. Pipes traveled the ceiling and poured water into a lone pipe teetering above my face. Kuval stood over me and searched my eyes. His lust made me uneasy. Why the hell would anyone desire something like me?

He pointed to the contraption over my head. "This is a bamboo water fountain. Do you know what that is?"

Ignorant about the fountain, despite my vast travels, I clenched my teeth determined not to say anything.

Kuval shrugged. "Wait just a moment, and you'll find out what it does."

"I'm not afraid of the sound of running water."

"Truly, you are brave." Kuval snickered. "The last to set foot in here pleaded all his fortune to me after the fourth cycle." He gestured at me. "Water only incensed you. This should be fun."

Flicking my wet hair back and forth, I yelled, "Bastard, throw water on me all you want, but stay the fuck away from me."

He laughed. "Let's play a game."

I was beginning to dread the twinkle in his eyes. "Go to hell."

"But that's the name of the game." He smiled and leaned against the laboratory table, pointing to a round metal spigot. "If you look close at this handle, it has notches. Each notch represents a minute. For each question you answer truthfully, I'll turn the knob and give you an extra minute."

"Ask away," I muttered.

"Oh, but I didn't *say* what that extra minute gets you." He looked up at the contraption high over my head.

A sense of dread, and my stomach didn't just drop, it scurried as far away from my middle as possible. This wasn't going to be good.

"Yes, I think you'll find out in. . . three, two, one."

The spout of the fountain started moving down. I saw the open mouth of the bamboo neck tilt down, and water poured from its mouth. Water reached its crest like fingers pointing at me. The slow fall of the liquid's torment sent a shiver down my spine. Then like an arrow going through my chest, the water hit. Water scorched me with its hate for

Fúrr, the Fire element inside me. My skin sizzled. It felt like the water tried ripping me open. It took me a moment to gain enough air to scream. My throat ached, and my voice went hoarse from my shriek.

When the cascade was over, I thrashed. My free legs were shoved down and locked. Metal pinned my ankles. My entire backside burned. The soaked coat and shirt clung to my body. Wet cloth sent lightning up and down my skin. I was being fried.

"Are you ready for questions?" Kuval's voice became my focus. Anything to escape the pain.

"Yes!" I panted, immediately biting my tongue for my weakness.

"Hmmm. This might not be as much fun as I thought. Still, a truthful answer if I ever heard one." He turned and eased the spigot a notch. His wince at the touch the only indication he was hurting from the burns on his hands.

Ashamed of my relief for an extra minute, I clenched my teeth. If I lied to myself, I might say I would be determined not to speak, but I wasn't a liar.

"Who sent you to kill me?"

I sighed and turned my head away. He wouldn't believe the truth, and I wasn't inclined to tell him.

"Oh, fuck, yes," Kuval said.

Turning my head back in question, I saw the bulge in his pants. I threw my head back and shut my eyes. "You sick bastard."

I heard a long-suffering sigh. "It's not your pain I find attractive. It's your strength."

Too afraid not to keep him in sight, I watched him lift up my book and turn the pages. Shit. He was waiting for the bamboo stick to fall again.

"You have to the count of ten to answer for a reprieve." Kuval flipped pages.

Running water from above filtered to the thin container. The hollow sound of the element pushing air out of the contraption's neck went silent, and the counterweight paused before pouring a million daggers my way. The extra minute wasn't a relief—it was prolonged torture.

Soon enough, the mouth of the fountain swung its way down. My breathing started to hitch. No. This wasn't happening. I wasn't going to keep my silence for long. I gasped. Water-soaked clothes grabbed at me. Pain sliced through my body. My shirt clung as if bonded onto my skin. Steam rose from my chest. My Fire was dying. I was dying.

"Ahhhhrghhhhh!" Already my throat had turned dry from screaming. No, I wasn't going to last.

He looked up from the book. "Who sent you?"

"Not my guild master."

"Oh, that's just cheating." He turned the knob another notch.

"I came by myself."

"You don't play the game very well." He turned more pages of the book. "I was going to ask who you were working with next to give you another minute, but since you volunteered, I'll have to think of another question."

"No big deal." I tried to sound calm.

He laughed. "Oh, I could fall for you."

Can I retch now?

"For what it's worth, Zeroh, I do like you, and I regret having to do this."

I looked at him, but all I saw was his back. He was flipping the pages of the book seemingly skimming the read.

"You don't have to do this." I tested the chains.

He didn't turn around.

"Hey!" I struggled with my bonds. "Look at me."

"No," he whispered.

"Go ahead, you bastard, kill me."

Kuval shook his head. "You'll live."

"Fuck. . ."

The water came crashing down. Droplets flung every which way splattering my legs, arms, and the top of my forehead. The tiny drops seared me like hot grease escaping from a pan. I screamed. This time my voice went completely hoarse.

Kuval cringed the entire time I was screaming. His next question came. "A name. Give me a name."

I gasped, choked, and turned my head to him. "His name is—" I choked on the small amount of water that crept in. Kuval crept toward me, eyes intent. I continued, "His name is, fuck you."

The ends of his lips curved slowly up, and his chest puffed out. The proud stance of a father looking upon his victorious son. But there was nothing "fatherly" about the want in his eyes.

"Zeroh. We've only got you up four notches. I started you at two-minute intervals. It's now at four-minute intervals. That's fifteen times an hour, you'll endure purifying water. Don't you want to make it easier on yourself?"

"Ask easier questions."

He huffed, "For all I know you weren't told who ordered the kill."

I clamped my mouth shut. It was better for him to think that.

"Well." He shrugged. "Easier questions then. I don't know how much you can take, and I'm not going to be here long."

"You're leaving?" A spike of panic shot through my middle.

"Yes."

"With the water on?"

"Yes." He turned his face away.

"If you can't take torturing me, then let me go."

He huffed, "To leave you free to kill me?"

Well, there was that.

"If you care to give me the contact's name I'll turn it off."

No. Arkenu deserved better from me. Aleenia was the first place in all of Iraythow I'd been able to stay. I owed that all to Arkenu, my guild master. There was honor among thieves, but if you were a Pyromage, no honor existed. Not for someone like me. But Arkenu had taken me in, made me a part of his inner circle, trained me, helped me. I owed him, and I wanted to prove to the guild I was one of them.

Water came down. I'd hoped I would become numb. The pain didn't recede. I sputtered, held my breath, but nothing worked. I screamed before the water fell over my chest. Droplets singed my tongue. I coughed and steam escaped my mouth.

Kuval held the book to my face. He had it on the same page I had studied at the bar. "What is this?"

The name of the knife was written above the illustration. "It's the Devil's Dagger," I panted.

He absently turned the spigot another notch while holding the book upside down.

"You can't read, can you?"

He leveled his gaze at me. "What does the Devil's Dagger do?"

I choked a laugh. "You can't read!"

"Most of Iraythow can't read." He shrugged. "So, what does it do?"

His lack of response to my insult cowed me. Absurd as it was, I felt like the asshole. "The book says it opens the door to hell."

He turned the book and looked at it curiously. He did not turn the spigot. The water tumbled down. Trying to hold my breath, I failed and sputtered a scream.

Kuval turned the knob and gazed at me. "For a smart, resourceful kid, you don't seem wise to my legendary repertoire."

"Says the man who's *reading* a book upside down."

"There is no book on street smarts. Reading doesn't make you intelligent."

"Reading gives you the ability to think without having to rely on someone else."

He pursed his lips and thought. "Hmmm. Haven't thought of it that way." He broke out of his reflection. "Out of curiosity, what's your caste?"

"Caste?"

"Yeah. Red, blue, or white? I bet you're a rare."

"I don't know what the hell you're talking about."

"Really?" Kuval came closer, looking down at me like I was a science experiment. "Does that mean you're a dragon with no caste?"

"I'm not a dragon."

"Yes, you are."

"No, I'm not."

"You really believe that," he murmured.

"I'm not a dragon."

"Showing you the truth is going to be so gratifying."

Water ripped at my chest. He'd kept me engaged enough to forget about the impending pain.

"One more question before I leave."

Oh, God. How many minutes in between waterfalls?

"Who wants me dead?"

I closed my eyes. The answer was me. Not that I had a grudge against him. It was my own idea to go after him. He was a mark, an initiation, my self-proclaimed goal. If I killed Kuval, Arkenu would have to see me as someone who was worth his time.

"Well, we can work on that." He turned the spigot another notch. "Eight," he said. "In case you were wondering."

Kuval stepped close and pulled my upper half up. He undid my cuffs behind my back. I would have punched him in the jaw if my limbs weren't uselessly numb. Instead, he laid me on my back and set my wrists in the clamps above my head attached to the stone altar.

"Since you don't want me to take off your wet clothes, I'll just leave them on." He gazed down into my eyes. "Comfortable?"

"No."

His lip quirked. "You sure you want to wallow in wet linen?"

I narrowed my eyes. "Yes."

He went to the spigot and turned it two more notches. He was leaving.

"Wait! You don't need this contraption to keep me here."

"It's in case you decide suicide is a better option."

"What?"

He pointed up. "You might decide to burn the ceiling. All of Aleenia's water supply would come crashing down. You'd die from Water burns before drowning."

"I won't." Tempting.

"I'd rather not take that chance." He turned to the door and, without looking back, said, "Every ten minutes, Ze-roh."

Fuck. How long was he going to be? "See you when you get back." My voice wasn't as strong as I'd like. "Pick up some eggs and milk."

Kuval bust out laughing. "Treating me like a bitch already? Just remember, you're the asshole trying to kill me."

CHAPTER 4

ELDYN

THE HALLS OF BROGAN Prison vibrated with a chaotic energy I'd never experienced before. Not even from an Ether dragon. It felt like madness. That's what it had to be. A dragon gone mad. Or worse. A black caste dragon. I shivered at the memory of meeting my first black caste Ethragon.

"So, your plan is to imprison me until I give up the dagger?" I looked to Arkenu who walked ahead of me.

We weren't alone. Others scurried behind us. They were either newbies practicing their shadow movements or intimidators purposefully scuffing their feet to let me know they were there. Either way, they were lucky I was more a laid-back pacifist than an uptight red caste.

"Think of it as more like protecting my future."

"By threatening my assistant?" I might be averse to violence, but if he hurt Thomas, my dragon half might be convinced to *rend* out of hiding. Not that I'd ever transformed before, but I'd be angry enough to try.

"He is my insurance." Arkenu stepped into what looked more like an office than a cell. Steel bars blocked a window in the shape of a half moon. The fall breeze sent a chill into the room. A wood desk and chair sat in front of a floor-to-ceiling shelf, full of books. Otherwise the room was empty.

I stepped inside, wondering if holding out was the wise decision. "How long do you plan to keep me here?"

Arkenu appraised me with snake-dead eyes. "You're wondering if I'll kill your apprentice if you don't give me what I want."

"He's not my apprentice, but yes."

"Despite what is needful, I'm not blood thirsty. Life is precious."

"Yet you murder people."

Leather creaked as his fist flexed and relaxed. "I remove obstacles for the greater good."

"And Thomas is just collateral damage." I raised my chin in challenge.

"He is an innocent." Arkenu gave an economic wave of his hand. "For now."

"Meaning you won't kill him?" Did he understand the definition of aegis? The very title he was given. *Protector, my scrawny ass.*

Arkenu crossed his arms and leaned against the door frame. "People are going to wonder where you are. When Thomas cannot provide your whereabouts, sales will drop. And when his shop owner doesn't pay him, Thomas will raid the store and sell what's left. When that runs out, he'll then find new work. Other shop owners might find his knowledge. . . helpful." The master assassin paused, watching my face with intense focus.

If he was waiting for a "tell," I wouldn't give him one.

He righted himself and reached for the door handle. "I see. He's truly a co-worker and not your apprentice then."

But his words gave me a revelation. Arkenu didn't understand magic. If he did, he'd know Thomas was not capable of wielding the elements. Neither was Arkenu for that matter.

Only those with God-blood such as drakes and dragons obtained the ability to cast magic. Drakes with less than ten percent dragon lineage could manipulate the elements but were mostly human. Full-blooded humans held no magic. A lower percentage of God-blood meant even drakes were essentially human and were considered mundane. Thus, humans never understood how some possessed powers while others did not. If they ever tracked their ancestry obsessively as drakes had, they'd have come to find out who had God's blood and who came from monkeys.

"I didn't lie." I acted offended. "Thomas is an employee."

"Only pure dragons behold themselves to honesty," he smirked, stepped out of the room, shut the door, and slid home a bolt lock.

"Jerk." He was trying to goad me.

I wanted to scream. Tell him off. But debating the lineage of drakes would give him too much knowledge. I turned my attention to the bookshelf and started fumbling through the tomes, waiting till Arkenu left. His dark gaze watched me through the bars of the door.

Fine. I could wait. Especially with such intriguing reads.

Lost Time was a book speculating the powers a dragon held over time manipulation. Human speculation of course. Dragon's did not jump space and time; it just looked that way.

Agog was another book written—by humans—about ancient dragon relics. The Devil's Dagger would not be noted in that book because the knife was much older than ancient. Much like how I felt sometimes. Looking for my intended mate was exhausting. I'd finally decided to stop traveling and stay still because if he were looking for me and wandering about, how likely was it that we'd meet up? So, a book shop and relics dealer was good as any other profession.

But I caught a glimpse of a newer book.

Relics of Casflamir.

Casflamir. I had not heard that name in so long I thought the curse of a man was gone from everyone's memory. Surely, he was dead.

When I looked back at the door, the eyes of perdition were gone. This was my chance. Time was not on my side. I crept up to the window and made sure Arkenu was truly gone. Nothing but an empty hallway stood between me and freedom.

I reached in my robe and pulled out the relic that had gotten us in this mess. The Devil's Dagger was said to have a thief's abilities. Time to see if those myths were true.

Thank you so much, Kuval. I relish the chance to have you dump this crap on me only to be jinxed by the knife's burden. The blade had the reputation of everyone wanting it and no one being able to keep it. Well, not everyone wanted this status symbol. I used the point as the lever to lift the hammers inside the keyhole, but before I could pick the lock, it unlatched.

"Huh, no wonder your wielders couldn't be held captive." The knife was its very own magic locksmith. Useful. Dangerous. Sneaky.

I opened the door and stepped out. A shadow leaning up against the wall pushed off and blocked my path. "That didn't take long." The voice of the shadow wasn't one I recognized. "Ian, alert Master Aegis."

Another shadow slinked away. Damnable. I had no idea who Arkenu had left to guard me, but they wouldn't be a paltry errand boy.

"Get out of my way." I pointed the knife towards him.

"Oh, by all means, try and make me." The shadow stepped back into the dark.

I was tempted to see what the knife would do. Speculation said it would turn the unworthy into demons. But that had to be a human's recollection of an Impart—when a dragon took their God-form for the first transformation. Things often went ugly. Humans often associated demon with dragon.

What I knew of the knife was much crueler. I set the Devil's Dagger back inside my robe for safe keeping. I didn't need weapons to dispatch an assassin.

Vesi came to my aid. All life contained water, especially the human shadow blocking my way. Humans were certainly a force to recon with, but they didn't have protection from magic. I pulled on the water pockets inside the shadowed guard. Time to find out a little more about their

Fire mage. "Did you know that victims of Hydromages and Pyromages look almost exactly the same?"

Even in the shadows, I saw him pause. His hesitancy was not just in my favor for information but necessary. Water magic was notoriously slow. But Water was loyal. Fierce. There was no question it would come, just a matter of when.

"You see, a Pyromage burns the body leaving—ash. A Hydromage pulls water from the body—leaving ash. You might wonder the difference between that pile of dust. Do you want to feel the difference?" I paused, letting the magic build, holding the water inside waiting for Vesi to crest.

He didn't answer me. Good, I was still stalling. "I'll tell you. It's pain. See, with Pyromages, there's a bit of heat, a flash, and then you're burned before you know it. Hydromages. . . well, we aren't such a kind lot. Still waters run deep, as they say, and the deeper the water, the colder it gets. Can you feel it yet?" Vesi rose, and I yanked the water in his body towards me, calling the liquid to leave its vessel. To flow free once more.

The guard started coughing. He was not experienced with Hydromages. He wouldn't have let me talk if he knew what I could do. Regardless, I couldn't regret what I was doing. Thomas and his family were on the line. I had to get out of here, get my assistant and his kin to safety, leave Aleenia, and go someplace else.

"Eldyn, you disappoint me." Arkenu stepped from the shadows as if he'd been there all along.

My concentration with Vesi wavered.

"I'm alerted whenever that door opens," Arkenu said.

Damnable. I bet this whole place was booby-trapped. But I held one of his own hostage. "Let me go, Master Aegis."

Arkenu stepped forward, out from the shadows. His face a hard mask of intolerance. "In the end, your human side still takes precedence and dishonors your word. You promised to come."

The jab spurred my ego. "I never promised not to escape."

The guard behind Arkenu went down to his knees. A splash hitting the stone floor accompanied a retch from behind the Aegis. Liquid, probably blood, started vacating the guard.

"Do you know what this is?" Silver flashed between Arkenu's fingers. He was holding a scarab. Not a real beetle, but an artifact. And, yes, I did know what it was and what it could do. Death by enchanted scarab was a nasty demise.

"Where did you get that?"

Arkenu laid the bug in his palm. "So, you know that all I have to do is whisper a name to it, and no matter where that person is, it will find them. Do you know what happens after that?"

"Do you?"

He smiled, and it was not sympathetic. "First, it crawls inside your head." He waved his large hand. "Through the nose, an ear, or even an open mouth. It doesn't matter. The pain as it eats its way to the skull I've heard is excruciating. Then its victim goes mad as it eats their brain."

Enough said. Except that if the scarab wasn't destroyed by the time the person died, it flew back to its master to be used again. Once the beetle was inside someone, the victim should be killed. It was the only way to prevent the torture.

"I'll take my chances." I flicked my wrist.

The guard sputtered and coughed. A pool glistened red in what little light illuminated the hall.

"Oh, no, Eldyn, you misunderstand me. I would not whisper your name."

He left out the specifics. My mind played on his taunt. Thomas. Kuval. Anyone I cared about. I couldn't be sure how much he'd found out about my past. What he knew. Not completely.

"Leave Thomas and his family out of it," I spat.

"You leave me no choice. Stop strangling my associate and return to your accommodations, or I send off this gift."

"That isn't real." I flipped my hand to the beetle. "It's probably just a pendant." He was bluffing. An enchanted scarab was so rare I had only come across one other. Its magic had been drained leaving only a pretty bobble that served as a paper weight. Being a dealer in magic, I'd seen my share of the forgotten, unusual, and extraordinary. The beetle was a priceless item. What pissed me off more was he hadn't acquired it from me.

Arkenu raised his hand and blew on the scarab. It's eyes glowed. Hidden wings sprung up from its back and fluttered. The bug turned around in his hand and searched with his head. . . waiting.

"Once I say the name, I cannot take it back."

I swallowed. It was an enchanted scarab. Even the one I came across in my shop hadn't been able to awaken. The beetle in Arkenu's hand became alive, crawling, searching, and buzzing its wings.

"Let my man go, wise one. Your round of heroics is over. The best course for your assistant and his family is for you to go back inside the room and wait."

Damnable. His careful choice of words shivered down my spine. My hold on Vesi lessened. The guard stopped losing "water."

"Make it dormant." I stepped back in good faith.

Arkenu glanced at the guard behind him. The man waved from his kneeling stance and started breathing easy. The guild master focused on the scarab and clucked. The beetle turned to him and waved its little head as if saluting.

"Sleep," Arkenu said, and his breath turned to frost as it rolled over his palm.

The beetle relaxed and resumed its original pendent-like stance.

My heart froze. Arkenu was human. That wasn't magic. Couldn't be. It was something else, but not magic. There was no forgotten son. No savior of the dragon race. No one person to help the drakes and humans become friends once more. No leader to guide our planet like a ship in this giant universe to where it should be. I'd looked. Searched. Spent half my life wandering, chasing strings of a prophecy that probably wasn't coming true.

Arkenu tucked away the scarab and stepped forward. I let go of Vesi, and my captive breathed easy. Once the guard stood back up, I stepped back, turned, and walked into my cage. The guild master of Kenwald followed.

He shut the door and stared at me while my heart pounded. My attempt to get out and save the people I cared about had failed. I expected retribution. Torture. For the interrogation to begin.

Arkenu only stood there.

Finally, I looked into his hard, cold eyes. I'd strained his patience, but his voice remained smooth as he said, "The moment you open this door, you'll be in breach of our agreement."

To save Thomas, I needed to comply. I bowed my head and remained silent.

"You have my word," Arkenu said, stepping to the door. "Stay in this room, and no harm will come to you or your co-worker."

"Your word as an assassin?"

"As the Aegis."

I let out a sigh of hopelessness and nodded. He was the Aegis, Protector of the realm, but I questioned whether he protected the citizens of Aleenia or his own interests.

"Say it, Eldyn."

"On my God-blood honor, I will remain in this room unless harm comes to Thomas, his family, or myself."

He grunted approval. "That I accept as a dragon's promise."

Arkenu closed the door, and this time, he didn't slide the bolt. There was no need to lock the door. My word was a matter of dragon pride. All my musings of escape left with the Kenwald Guild Master.

CHAPTER 5

ZEROH

A SINGLE WATER DROPLET hung from the chain threatening its descent towards my chest. I'd lost track of how many times the pipe turned its mouth down and splattered a thousand agonizing knives through my gut, my chest, and my legs. My skin no longer sizzled when the water poured over me. But the pain of being that barrier between two warring elements took its toll. I'd blacked out twice. Each time becoming cognizant just before another bout of water hurled itself onto my body.

"Please," I croaked, my voice shredded from all the screams of previous dowsings. I was down to begging the elements to be kind. Begging to stop an eon-long war between Fire and Water. In the silent dark, I heard disembodied whispers. "Our apologies, brother," they said, but their remorse did not sound sincere. "But we will extinguish you."

Delirious. I'd become delirious. Water spoke. Why not? Even my own Fire communicated to me. Not in words but in the shapes of its flame.

"I'm not part of your war," I cried.

"You think not?" The combined, disembodied voices held a lisp of contempt.

The sound of the bucket overhead made low-pitched sounds indicating the tub was almost full, and the pipe would soon release the collected water.

"Please!" I twisted trying to move out of the direct hit. Exhausted and drained of hope, my body didn't actually move. Thin burning strands of water, where the metal pinned me at my wrists and ankles, seeped into the cloth and cut at my skin. A pool, settled in the hollow of my throat, felt like acid eating away at my Adam's apple. The single droplet, hanging from the metal chain, finally let go and dropped down. . . down. . . down. . .

A hammer blow hit the side of my face. One single drop of water left me numb and disoriented.

"No more," I rasped. "I'm sorry," I said to my element. At least, we would die on a mission. I'd failed Arkenu.

The next bucket would send me unconscious. I doubt I'd wake up from one more bucket of punishing torment. Thoughts climbed into my mind, trying to separate from the agony. Unfortunately, the pain of a lifetime was my company. The first memory of not being normal sat next to me on my bench of hurt. That bench held all the memories of a single incident that destroyed my life. His name was Vavar.

I watched as the pipe began its slow descent to lowering liquid pain. The rattle of keys, the creak of a door. . . was it Kuval? The pipe lowered. The wave of a waterfall started its way downward. My heart raced. I was going to die.

Then I saw the bottom of a wood bucket. The round pail blocked my view of the coming tide. Kuval was right. I wanted to face my enemy, not be blinded from it.

"Whew, that was close," Kuval said.

The wood bucket was gone, but my hazy eyes stayed locked on the bamboo pipe.

A metal squeak from the wall reverberated through the room. But the deafening sound of water rushing through pipe didn't die. My breathing hitched.

"Zeroh," Kuval said.

I blinked and his face ruled my vision. "Shit, Zeroh, your eyes. Your eyes. . . they've gone dark."

My eyes? Gone dark? Was the Fire blazing in my pupils gone? "What color are my irises?"

I'd forgotten the true color of my eyes. In my youth, when I was a normal human with normal eyes, I hadn't cared. Now, the Fire that blazed around my pupil was a sour reminder of my power, my mistakes, and my public ostracizing.

"Zeroh!" Kuval yelled into my ear. "Flame up, man. Come on. I'm right here. Don't you want to finish what you started?"

His hands pressed into my skin, and I wailed. It was as if hot pokers had pierced my skin.

"Shit." Kuval set me down.

There were sounds like someone rummaging in a trash can. He pushed me on my side and unlocked the metal cuffs around my wrists. My hands and legs were free, but my limbs weighed me down, stinging the numbness out. I winced at the water sliding down my hands. My body didn't respond to me anymore. Hell, even if I did have feeling in my limbs, my will to fight was ash in the wind.

Kuval lifted me in a sitting position, my arms flopped at my sides. The tingling stumps were too heavy to control.

He tugged at my clothes. Cutting my skin clean off, or that's what it seemed. Whimpers scorched my throat. My only protest was a moan of distress.

"I'm sorry. I have to get this off."

Soft cotton wrapped around my back. The towel soaked up the water, lifting it away, but my element's enemy was still too close to my skin. He wrapped another towel over my head. I hissed as if being scalped. I tried to scream. All that came out were heavy pants of frustration.

"Flame up!" Kuval said. "You wanted to kill me. Now's your chance. Come on, Zeroh."

His voice became my focus away from pain.

"The only way you're going to live is if you fucking burn. Come on, Zeroh. Let me see your Fire."

Is that what he meant by flame up? I didn't have enough energy to give my *Fúrr*. My insides shredded, used up. Every ounce of my fight had staved off Water. Now, there was nothing left.

"Sleep," I said. Let me sleep.

Kuval's voice grew frantic. "No! Not allowed. Come on, damn you. You can't sleep."

My head jerked and a mild sting bloomed across my cheek.

"Sleep," I begged. Boulders sat on my eyelids.

"Fuck!" Kuval shouted. "Hey, hey! Open your eyes. Zeroh. . . shit, shit, shit. . . kid, come on, fight."

My body shook and consciousness started fading.

"Kid! I'm sorry, but I can't think of anything else."

A writhing, desperate eel found its way into my mouth as Kuval stuck his tongue down my throat. An hour ago, I would have melted his face off. Powerless to stop it anyway, I allowed his kiss. Hell, have at it if that's what he really wanted. I tentatively searched with my own probing tongue. The sensation wasn't unpleasant. He wasn't disgusting. Far from it. I didn't ponder more on the matter and met him with lips and tongue as our teeth clashed together.

Kuval pulled back. "Come on, man. Aren't you angry? Was all your bluster of *I'm not into men* bullshit?"

I didn't say I wasn't into men. I'd said I wasn't into you. "Sleep." The inner protest was lost in my delirium. My body sank into Kuval's chest.

"Damn it, boy. How many times do I have to tell you? Flame up, or you're going to die!"

No amount of name-calling would make my fingers work to flip him the bird. "Fuck off."

He slipped his tongue into my mouth, and I let him. The sensation was rather unique. Pleasant. Anything to get away from the pain.

Please, no more Water trying to rip me inside out. But I possessed no more energy to reciprocate his kiss. He still teased in a desperate attack. His hand slipped to my stomach and my cock twinged. How unexpected. I became more aware of what was happening. I didn't care. Anything to continue this pleasurable haze. Anything but the pain of Water.

"Don't you want to burn me?" Kuval pressed a cloth that soaked up the rest of the water off my body. "You said you'd fry me for doing this to you. So, go ahead and try."

Mouth open and panting, I gazed at him. If I had more energy, I might coax his tongue back inside. The sensation of melding with another human being felt right. How long had it been? At least, I wouldn't die alone.

His hand traveled south of my waist and brushed my cock. It was the most exquisite feeling. After being pounded with pain, I welcomed anything pleasurable. With my legs spread, I could only move so much, but I tried rubbing up against his hand. His fingers explored my sac and rimmed my puckered anus.

"I've never been so desperate to be proven wrong." Kuval shifted me, giving him better access to my back end. "If you don't stop me, I'm going to slide my finger up your ass. Come on, Zeroh. Get angry."

Stop the only thing feeding my Fire? Never.

"Come on, kid. Hello? Do you know what I'm doing?" His words were desperate. Pleading. Asking me to come back to the world of the living.

No, thanks. Not if death was this good.

"I'm going to continue, so you better wake the fuck up." Our mouths connected again. He laid me flat on the stone, kissing me all the way down. His wrist grazed over my stiffening rod. A gauze-wrapped hand started stroking my cock. No reaction, but then again, I was dying. His kisses turned from desperate to eager.

"Kid, what do I have to do to get you mad?" Kuval proved his sexual finesse from his lips to his handling. Fingers skimmed my sides. His tongue went deeper and slowed its pace. It was as if he was opening me up. Taking me in. Using this chance to get inside me.

His knees straddled my hips. The dead weight of my arms tingled alive. He took the towel off my head, threw it aside, and bunched a dry sheet and set it behind me to use as a pillow.

I gazed up at him in utter contentment. My Fire gained momentum, smoldering in my gut. A tiny spark held onto the faintest string of emotion.

"Zeroh! Come on, kid."

He was starting to piss me off. I wanted to feel good. Whatever he was doing, this attention he gave me, his desperate voice, the touching of skin to skin, all sent my Fire lines of hope. Hope burned slow, building in a fragile strength raging up into the sky smoldering within a single touch.

"Get angry, damn you." My cock thickened at Kuval's five-fingered perusal. The soaking-wet towel went away, replaced by a dry one. His hand, vigorously pumping my rod, was dry. As I lingered in the haze, an urge I'd promised myself to never let loose rose from the base of my core. I hummed at human contact. This feeling was so foreign, yet familiar. Desire. Lust. A memory.

Dark eyes hovered over my imagination. Vavar crouched on his knees. His mouth on my skin where no one had ever touched melted my knees. A column of ecstasy rushed through me. But when I opened my eyes, my hometown was on fire. Everyone I loved, my parents, all my friends. . . everyone was on fire. No one survived. And it was all my fault. My fault for letting go. For lusting after another person. Setting the magic within me free.

I snapped my eyes open. "No!"

"Right," he said. "Come on, Sparky. Burn."

He threw my arms above my head and clamped them in the altars cuffs. My ankles were already back in the lower confinements. In a burst of combustion, flame surrounded me. My Fire sparked back up.

Fúrr used the memory of an old pain as kindling. That alone kept my Fire stoked. Never again would I kill another human being in *that* way. Not even Kuval. It was no easy feat, but he'd saved my life. Probably in the only way that would work.

Kuval stepped back and sighed in relief. "Good job, kid."

I let my Fire rage while Kuval watched me with eager eyes.

His hands trembled and the proud, strong man that captured me seemed much less confident. Remorseful. Disturbed. Hurt. "I'm sorry. I didn't mean. . . It was all I had to get you back."

This wasn't the man that would bring me notoriety. This man was human. Layered in mystic. I wanted the smiling Kuval back.

"Thank you," I whispered.

For the life of me, I wouldn't be able to tell if my gratitude lay in saving my life or for giving me a taste of passion once more.

Kuval slunk over to a chair and sat with his back to me, head in his hands. He stayed that way for a while until the wood ceiling formed a dry patch.

"Simmer down, Sparky." Kuval stood and gazed down at me. "You won't damage the rock but don't set fire to the ceiling." He rapped a knuckle on the wood above him and winced. "Damn." He looked at his hand. "I have to admit, you got me good. This is not going to be pleasant."

Soaking in my Fire was too tempting. It hadn't been long, but the separation between *Fúrr* and I seemed like an eternity. My Fire burned with an age-old fury that had little to do with me and more about being extinguished by Water. Fúrr's rage alone fueled its own flames.

But it wasn't long before Water droplets started seeping between the dried planks.

"Zeroh," Kuval admonished. "The wood expands when it's wet and can't keep the water in. If you dry the ceiling, there's going to be a leak."

While I brought the flames around me to an early morning camp fire, Kuval pulled out a vial with glowing pink liquid inside. With wrapped hands and a dainty touch, he held the vial as if it would burn him.

"What the hell is that?"

"Nu-skin." He set the vial in a holder. He breathed in as if psyching himself up to face a pack of demons. His sole focus was on that pink liquid.

"What's Nu-skin?"

That question earned me a look. A look that proclaimed me stupid.

"You really are fresh out your egg, aren't ya?" Kuval shook his head. "Damn, kid, how old are you?"

"Twenty-one," I snapped.

He choked. "Well, I'll be."

The smile I received sank my heart down a dark, deep well. I didn't want to examine what I found there.

"So are you a virgin; is that your issue?"

Indignation got the better of me. "What does that have to do with anything?"

Kuval grinned like the devil's older, more debonair brother. "So, yes, you're a virgin."

"I'm not completely clueless." My Fire licked around my sides, burning a bit higher.

"So, you're used to strangers doing what they want with you and that's not why you were able to get angry." He pumped his arm in the air in the unmistakable masturbating motion.

"Shut up." He might have saved me, but I didn't owe him answers.

"Did I pop your cherry?"

"I said shut up."

His voice dropped into a murmur. "Did you like it?"

"Fuck you."

The smile on his face held a remorseful quality until he turned back to the vial. The gauze on his hands was tinted in brownish-red stains. He gingerly unraveled the wrapping. Pain radiated off his face as strips of cloth peeled from his hands. Burnt flesh and stagnant septic rankness overshadowed the room's oppressive wet musk.

Blood and dead skin stuck to the cloth as Kuval exposed shriveled-up fingers resembling bloody, oozing sticks. I'd done that. I'd burned him. He'd also used his hands on me to save my life.

"Hurts, doesn't it?" A small consolation for the torture he had put me through wrapped around my guilt. The blame game would go round and round, but the truth was I had started this path of mutual destruction.

His eyes flicked up. "Yes," he sneered. "Be prepared. Payment for saving your life shall be extracted through that body of yours."

The diabolical thief of the Vandfald clan glowered at me. Here I was, chained to a stone table, laid out for his perverted pleasure, and I was mouthing off as if I had the upper hand.

Kuval smiled, wiping off his dangerous expression. He winced at peeling off the last layer of cloth sticking to his oozing hand.

"Guess that's what I get for playing with an adolescent dragon."

"I'm not adolescent. Or a dragon."

He ignored me, pinched the lip of the vial, uncorked the container, and stood with his eyes closed. Kuval took deep breaths before opening his eyes again. Walking to a bucket of water he heaved breaths like he was preparing to skin dive to the bottom of the ocean. He plunged his unwrapped hand into the water and grunted. A second later, he pulled his hand out. More controlled breathing. Then Kuval poured half the vial of pink liquid over his now wet hand.

Soon as the pink ooze hit his leftover skin, he started screaming. "Oh, fuck! Motherfucker! Fuck! Fuck! Fuck!" He breathed in and out, in and out, in and out. Kuval gulped another deep breath. He shrieked an ear-shattering scream and dropped to his knees holding his arm up.

"Motherfucker! Motherfucker!" he repeated. His tattoos rippled along his shoulders and arms. They looked like black lightning shifting down his body.

"The fuck?" I didn't want to watch his suffering.

Kuval's shaking head slowly rose until his sneer of hate ordained my eyes. The taste of his rage became palpable. Whiffs of pain crossed my nose. But it was his expression turned fury unto me that curdled my skin. Even *Fúrr* smoldered down barely skimming over my body. No wonder he was feared. That face would make an angry bull flee.

Teeth bared, he said, "It heals the skin."

He held out his shaking hand, the one he'd poured the pink goo over. A gel of red and flesh coalesced and stretched over his palm. Skin spread out over the tendons of his fingers, closing up around the meat of his hand. Why was he showing me this?

Shaking, eyes wide, teeth gritting, he started unwrapping the gauze from his other hand. His pain had to be excruciating. It was more than I could take just having gone through a similar torture.

He finished unraveling his other hand and underwent another torturous process. Soon as he poured the rest of the pink liquid on the other afflicted palm, the vial slipped from his grip. Glass shattered against the stone floor. Tiny sparkling shards skittered over the ground.

The cocky, ever-ready-with-a-quip Kuval was screaming for mercy. A full one-eighty from his larger-than-life attitude. Torture was not fun.

Being an assassin, a thief, or anything else Arkenu wanted me to be, my element was Fire. But even when I killed, there were no screams. Nothing like this. My Fire was too hot and too quick for anyone to scream. My *marks* were graced with instant incineration. The act took all of my concentration. It was why I couldn't just kill him on the spot in the alley or here. The process also wiped me out, but it was better than bloodcurdling screams. I made sure no pain befell most of my targets no matter how much effort it took. Here and then gone. That was my only saving grace. My kills were fast. If only to save the scrap of humanity left to me.

"Please stop," I whispered.

Kuval's agonizing confession, growing hoarse, brought back horrible memories. What the hell was he doing?

After my ears felt like they were bleeding, Kuval sat in the fetal position, head on his knees, hands around his waist. He'd stopped screaming and breathed.

"You're insane," I whispered. I doubt he heard me over his own clamoring. "The shock alone should've killed you."

"Maybe," his voice wheezed. "But Nu-skin is the only thing that rapid-heals burns."

"You can't read but you perform alchemy?"

Kuval grabbed a cup of water and drank. Sweat beaded off his half-naked body. "In a short time, you'll understand the consequences for burning me, and why I want to heal quickly as possible."

"Touch me and burn." I narrowed my eyes.

Kuval cast a smile down at me. "You're cheeky for someone in chains. I like you."

"Your affection scares me more than anything else," I huffed.

"Simmer down, Charcoal."

I turned up the flames covering my body.

"Nah-ah." He clucked and lifted the bucket of water. "Simmer down."

"Do I look like a hearth?" But I had no desire to go another round with Water. I decreased my flame.

"There's a good boy."

"Don't call me that."

Kuval stepped over and tweaked my nose. "Good boy."

If only I were a *good boy*. I wouldn't be in this mess.

After setting the bucket down, Kuval strode over to the door where he opened a burlap sack large enough to stuff a body inside. He pulled out a green glass bottle with a spout on top.

"Olive oil." He came over and sat in between my legs. Bottle in hand, his other palm held over my chest. "Simmer down a little lower."

I clenched my teeth. "What for?"

"Come on. Don't worry, Sparky, this won't hurt."

His bright smile made me pull at the metal bands around my wrists.

"Don't be like that. I've got something for my good boy."

"Ugh. Stop calling me that."

He stared at me. "Let's not pretend who's in charge here."

I blinked. The audacity. "It wouldn't be hard to kill you. Even strapped to this stone bed. You understand that, right?"

He smiled sweetly. "Oh, you're talking about the internal combustion trick?" He circled a finger above my stomach. "You melt a person's organs so fast they implode."

That was a secret technique. Something Arkenu had taught me.

"So, my only question is—why haven't you done that to me?" Kuval glanced at the ceiling answering himself.

Resigned, I closed my eyes and sighed. "Fine."

My Fire lowered, reducing my heat output.

Liquid hit my stomach. Olive oil oozed over my navel to my chest.

"What the hell?" It didn't hurt, but it was a surprise.

He answered with only a half-lidded seductive gaze and a knowing smirk. His hand hovered over my chest for about four seconds. Gutsy, considering I'd burned his hands and he'd just recovered.

"Perfect, stay like that." He went back to the burlap sack.

"No, I mean what the ever-loving, sick, twisted—what are those?"

Kuval laughed having pulled two white-wrapped packages. "Stop being so paranoid, kid."

"Stop calling me kid! Stop calling me good boy! Stop calling me degrading shit!" I pulled at all four bonds in an attempt to rid myself of my frustration. There was no way I was getting out. The metal clasps held me tight. Oil oozed over the sides of my chest and hips, making my skin slippery.

My warden unwrapped one package. "Stay still."

The succulent scent of prime beef may have caused a bit of drool to leave my lips.

Kuval took the package and slapped the rarest piece of steak I'd ever seen on my chest.

For the first half second, I lay in shock. Then I erupted. "I'm not a *fúrr* damn utensil. I'm not your fucking grill."

"Yes, you are." He pulled out another white package.

"You. . . bastard. . ." I started pulling at my bonds again.

"Stop." Kuval's command reverberated within the room and through my bones. "If you burn my food or dump it on the floor, I will eat your share."

"And if I ruin that one?" I sneered.

"I'll open the fountain wide open and go have a leisurely dinner somewhere across town."

I stopped moving. "You wouldn't dare."

"I'm not kidding. These were expensive, and I'm starving. You want to get in the way of a carnivore and a good piece of meat?" Our eyes held each other in challenge.

Then, the largest growl in the history of hunger pains rumbled through my stomach. Cowed—by my own body. Embarrassing.

Kuval laughed, unwrapped the other piece of meat, and slapped that chuck of prime beef along my stomach.

"Good thing you're paipan." He walked to the table and rummaged through tools.

"I'm not hairless." Fucker. I had *some* pubic hair. I lifted my head and looked down. Two large sides of cow beef blocked my view. But I didn't need vision to see my cock growing stiff. Over a meal no less.

He snorted. "I'm willing to wager you don't take care of yourself down there."

This growing hard-on needed to be dealt with, so I closed my eyes. Vavar's face appeared. No more stiffy. My cock shriveled up and went back to its soft state. It worked every time.

"When's the last time you ate?"

I had to think about the answer. "Yesterday?"

He came back with a pair of metal cooking clamps and my antique book. Kuval shook his head and sat down.

I jumped at my cock being squeezed between two metal prongs. "Hey!"

"Your dicks in the way."

Fúrr damn it. I'd just gotten rid of my hard-on only to have that part of me pop back up. "Can you refrain for five minutes?"

He flipped one of the steaks and flipped it back. "Just making sure you're not ruining dinner."

"I know how to maintain."

Kuval shrugged. Cooking clamps in hand, he opened the book with the other and settled on a random page. "Oh look! There's Yair." He pointed the utensil at an illustration of a gold dragon. The traditional kind with four limbs, two wings, a long neck, a long snout, a long tail, and glowing eyes.

"Yair is a legend," I huffed. "A bedtime story. And don't stain my book, you illiterate heathen."

He clucked his tongue. "Yair was the ruler of Aleenia a long time ago, way before the war. There are some that still remember him."

"If dragons are supposed to live forever, where is he now?"

"Ever heard the promise of the fire damned?"

"Great. Is this a don't play with fire story?"

Kuval settled down like he was going to tell me a long tale. "No. Actually, Yair was the only Pyragon to have a Hydromage rider."

"Oh, a fairy tale." Fire and Water elementals in the same room? Ha! Fire and Water working together? Never. Riders. Dragons. I'd never seen any. They were extinct or highly exaggerated.

He chuckled at me. "Yair loved his rider so much that he cast a blessing on himself. Stop me if you know this one."

"Whatever. Flip the meat, would ya?"

"Thanks." He snapped the book closed and used the clamps to turn the steaks over. Meat juice pooled around my ribs and navel. Good thing I could concentrate my heat over certain parts of my body or the wood ceiling might dampen our food—and me.

"So, what blessing?"

"Do you bless your food?" He gave a wry smile.

"No, come on, Yair blessed himself."

"Oh that. You didn't seem interested."

I rolled my head back and forth. "You're a sadist."

"You're a masochist. What a perfect match we make."

Breathing in, I went for humble patience. Not my strong point. "Please tell me." Otherwise his untold tale would niggle in my brain like nursing an aching tooth.

"Are you interested?"

I sighed and tried not to laugh while saying, "I like the sound of your voice. It's so masculine."

That did the trick. Kuval laughed. Egomaniac.

"Well, Yair blessed himself so that anything he loved would not be affected by his flame."

"Why?" How strange.

"Have you ever burned something you didn't want burned?"

Oh. That struck too close to home. I answered. Barely. "Yes."

A lump in my throat formed. I had burned something precious. Someone. He would never come back.

When Kuval said nothing, I turned my eyes in his direction. His solemn face offered pity. I wasn't deserving.

"Then you understand why," he said.

Yeah. Thinking about it, Yair probably had the right idea.

"But it backfired." His smile returned.

I rolled my head in disgust. The puns alone would kill me. Yet I was thankful. The heavy weight of memories lifted from my thoughts.

"How?" I said.

"He loved someone that didn't return the sentiment. In the end, he was murdered because he couldn't protect himself. His Fire didn't touch the very person that killed him."

"Moral of the story—don't love anyone."

"A bit jaded."

"I'm an assassin."

"That doesn't mean you're void of emotion."

Silence.

Kuval shuffled the steaks on my chest. "That's why I was wondering what caste you belong to."

"I'm not a dragon."

"Well, you're not a drake."

"What's the difference?"

He paused, gave me a once over, and shook his head. Score—one point. I stumped him.

"Off." He poked at my belly.

I sighed in disgust. Reduced to being a grill. Fantastic. I shut my Fire, *Fúrr*, down.

Kuval got up, put the book and the cooking clamps away, and brought back the biggest, sharpest knife I'd ever seen. The pommel was a beautiful pink-and-white rock. The blade swirled in a wavy pattern, but the edge was so thin I couldn't tell exactly where it ended. The weapon looked lethal.

My voice wavered. "Hey... I don't taste good."

He chuckled at me and sat by my side on the altar. "Don't worry, Charcoal. I'm good with a knife. You won't get cut. Just stay still."

Oh fuck, fuck, fuck. This was not going to go well. My body tensed in preparation. In my embarrassment, certain parts of my body stiffened from nerves.

"Sorry, but you'll notice this place doesn't have plates. Or cups. Or a stove." Kuval slid the knife over the cooked meat. The blade sank halfway with one slow slide into the meat on my chest.

I closed my eyes. No. No. No. This could not be my last night on Neith. I waited for the blade to cut into my skin. The pressure of the meat shifted. Kuval passed the knife over once more. Anytime now, he'd cut into me. I squeezed my eyes shut.

Pain never came. Moist, succulent flesh bumped my lips. I opened my eyes. Kuval pushed a thin piece of steak past my teeth and into my mouth. The meat dissolved with the wash of my saliva. A small chunk of beef was swallowed along with my disbelief. Not even a scrape on my skin. This time I watched. Only this time he started cutting the steak next to my own favorite piece of meat.

My view was obstructed by the dinner on my chest, but I waited for the slicing pain. Nothing. Kuval took a thin hunk of steak by the tip of the knife and slipped the food in his mouth. He didn't chew, only sighed and swallowed.

"Perfect, you're my grill for life."

The meat he picked was impressive. But not as impressive as his skill with a blade. The one *utensil* was all he used to feed us both. Again and again, I waited for him to cut into my flesh, to use the knife as an implement of torture. For blood to drip down my side. But he never so much as suggested he'd cut into me. He fed me slice after slice of the rarest meat.

"Relax, Sparky. Don't you know I'm really good with these?" He waved the blade in a circle.

"I noticed." My voice cracked. His boast seemed too much like a threat.

Kuval carefully sliced off another piece and fed me. He was right. The thief was not just good with a knife, he was a grand master. The tool was an extension of his fingers. There was not one slip of control. He cut the meat all the way through, and yet the blade never touched me. He proved his ability, cut after cut. But my tension never let up. It would be my luck to relax and then be sliced in half. Only at the last, and when I'd been stuffed with meat, did I let out a relieved breath.

My prison guard chuckled, licked the blade clean, and put the knife on the counter where he'd gotten it. Kuval came back and sat on his knees between my legs. That mischievous glint in his eye and his smirk of unnatural charm hinted he aimed to misbehave. What he had in store for the night would now be revealed. Shudder.

"So, we can do this the wet way, or the dry way." He brushed his finger along my chest and drew a squiggly pattern down to my stomach. Kuval sucked the juices off his fingers. He then licked his lips and leaned over me. His expression dared me to burst into flame. He was testing me. Finding out how I would react.

"You think feeding me will make me compliant?"

"Wasn't it good?"

"It was delicious." I narrowed my eyes.

"We'll try the dry way first." Kuval bent and lowered his face to my chest. "Burn me, and I'll open the pipes."

Kuval flicked his tongue over my right nipple. I jolted. Shit. My lower half twinged. He swiped over my pert bud again. My reaction was the same. He licked me from nipple to nipple, across my chest. I pulled on my restraints, knowing they wouldn't let me go. His tongue licked swaths of my front side. When the oil and juices were replaced by saliva, Kuval rose up and smoothed his hands over my chest and my sides from my shoulders to my navel, teasing my midsection.

Hands smoothed over my body. I squirmed under his touch. He brought his hands up and sucked what was left of the oil and juices from the meat. Those large hands enveloped me. They were large enough to wrap his fingers around my waist. Just the span of his forefinger and thumb was enough to choke me if he wanted. Then there was the matter of his physical touch. I'd denied myself the soft press of skin on skin for a long time. So long that this form of petting became uncomfortable.

My breath elevated. My heart tried hiding up in my throat. I wasn't used to connecting to another person. But here was Kuval, spreading his hands over my body. Licking the juices clean off my chest and sides.

"Easy, Sparky."

"Why are you doing this?"

"Just cleaning my grill."

I was getting used to his hands, his touch. Kuval was gentle. Slow. Testing every part of my chest. What scared me the most was not how wonderful this felt, or why I reacted to this man, or the softness in his eyes. No. The thing that was frightening was how much I was getting used to this feeling. How my guard dropped against his onslaught. The comfort I found in each stroke.

He was getting to know my body. His fingers glided up and down, circling in soothing lashes. The nerves along my sides also got used to Kuval's fingers sliding past. My muscles accepted his palms washing over me. His lips and occasional nips became welcome torments.

My cock reacted to his hands on my chest. His fingers massaged my waist all the way up to my ribs. His hands were slow, firm, and reassuring. Those same large hands rubbed down and grazed the tip of my boner. His smile returned with an irritating smugness.

"Shut up." I looked away.

"Oh, your first request." He slunk downward.

"What are you doing?" I lifted my head to look.

Kuval ignored me and pressed his lips against the middle of my erection. Lightning struck.

"The hell! Are you crazy?" I blurted.

He licked my member from base to tip. The shudder of pleasure racked me head to toe. Oh *fúrr*, that felt good.

"That's not wise." I clenched my teeth for his next barrage.

"Why? Was that your first kiss?"

"No, of course not," I huffed.

"By a man?"

I turned my head. "No."

"Ah, well, I was hoping to have your first. What happened to not liking men?" He licked my cock from base to tip again.

"Megalomaniac," I said through gritted teeth.

He chuckled. "Don't worry. I know all about Pyragon essence." He ran his tongue around the rim of my head.

"Please, wait." He was going to get a face-full of lava if he didn't knock it off.

"Relax, Sparky, I've got you." He ran his hands over my chest and lightly skimmed my nipples.

"Do you have a death wish?"

He pulled back. "You're the one in chains trying to kill me."

"Look, if you think my Fire burns, my cum disintegrates everything. This ceiling, stone, metal, everything, gone." And if everything burned, a ton of water from above was going to finish what the faucet of torture hadn't.

"Yeah, the Veteris made me memorize the creeds." Kuval stopped and rummaged around his person-sized burlap sack. "Don't make a Wind dragon laugh. Don't make an Earth dragon angry. Don't make a Water dragon cry, and don't make a Fire dragon cum." After reaching all the way down to the bottom, he pulled out a box case. "That's why I got these." He opened the box and pulled up a clear vial. There was nothing inside the tube.

"Glass?"

"A vial." He held the tube as if it were a prize from a king.

"What the hell are you going to do with that?"

"Remember when I said you'd pay with your body?" He pointed at my lower half. "You're going to fill it."

"With what?"

He rolled his eyes and pointedly looked at my middle.

Horror-struck. "Wait. What? Are you thinking of collecting my... my cum?"

"Yep."

"In that?"

"Yep."

"A glass vial is going to break the moment I pour any kind of my fluid in it."

He did a double take. "It's an essence vial."

I huffed, "Doesn't matter what you call it." What was he thinking?

Kuval, the great thief, dropped his jaw and looked at me like I was a naive dolt too old to be excused for my stupidity. "It's bottled Ether."

"What the hell is bottled Ether?"

"Okay, wait. . . time to be blunt." He waved his hand. "Let's start from the beginning." Kuval squatted beside me. "When's the last time you had sex?"

That was all it took to shut my body down. Vavar. My adoptive parents. My Friends. Neighbors. Everyone. Gone.

"Woah." Kuval eyed my middle. "That's impressive turtling." He examined my face. "This keeps bothering me. Dragons."

"I'm not a dragon."

"Kid, drop the act."

"I'm not a dragon."

Kuval sighed. "Okay. We'll set that aside for now." Even his pensive expression cast an alluring magnetism. "Where are you from?"

"Oh, okay. I once lived in a town called, fuck you."

Kuval smiled, but sadness tinged his eyes. "Zeroh, where did you grow up?"

Nobody had heard of the town I was from. It was so far north people spoke a different language. The place was gone as of six years ago. What did it matter if he told him the name of the place? "Burrow Hills. And thank you for bringing up a bitch of a memory, asshole." The urge to kick him made me try to test my bonds.

Kuval slowly closed his eyes. A pained expression clouded his handsome face. "Were you adopted?"

Was that a guess? But in reality, I'd never known my real parents.

"Answer, Zeroh." His impatience bordered on anger.

"Yes. I was adopted."

Kuval raked a hand through his hair. "Damn." He sighed. "Okay, the story goes like this. You were found as a baby, right?"

"I was saved from a monster."

"That's what you were told?"

"Yes."

"The people who found you took you in?"

"Whinny and Lily, my adoptive parents, killed the monster and saved me." Didn't do him any good in knowing about my family. They were all dead.

Kuval shook his head. "Zeroh. . . that monster was probably your birth mother or father taking you to Ekinphrow."

What the *fúrr*? He made no sense. "So, now you're trying to write my history."

"What was their name? The one you burned."

Our eyes met. He knew. I don't know how, but he knew. "Who?"

He shook his head. "What was his name? Or her name. The human you tried to have sex with?"

I looked away. No. My shame. The very thing that made me flee the only home I'd known. I wish I'd burned with them. But Pyromages don't burn.

"It's more common than you think." Kuval rested a hand on my arm. "So, you were saved by a monster that was probably your birth parent. You never made it to Ekinphrow. Never told what you were. Thought all this time you were human."

"Shut up." His words weren't true.

"Then you fell in love, lust, whatever. . ."

"You can stop."

"Yeah. The Fire-orphan stories are always awful. The element hits at puberty. Did he even know he was burning to death?"

"You son of a bitch!" I thrashed. The bonds kept me on the stone slab. "I'll kill you," I raged. Fire surrounded me until I couldn't see past the flames.

Water cut through my wall of plasma and hit like a hammer blow. The elements fought. I screamed. Tiny needles prickled my skin. I hurt until steam overtook the remaining Water.

Kuval stood at the foot of the altar ready with another water bucket. "Do you need another?"

"Go right ahead!" I snarled.

His hands stayed the bucket. "Burrow Hills still burns. Twenty Ethermages rotate preventing that particular fire from traveling south. Any time one of them lets up—it gains ground."

"That was six years ago."

Kuval leveled his gaze. "There is a sanction out for the dragon that started that fire."

All the energy whooshed out. That was me. I'd started that fire. Small flames came creeping over my skin waiting for Kuval to throw the Water in his hands. "Then claim your bounty, thief, because I'd rather be dead than spend another moment with you."

CHAPTER 6

ELDYN

"I COULD KILL YOU." I watched Arkenu search through books as if he were scanning for a certain passage.

"You could try." He opened a red leather-bound journal and flipped through its pages. "Hydromages are slow. I wouldn't give you time to build your energy."

There went that threat. "You'd be under the ocean before you knew it."

"As well as your assistant."

True. "You're not getting the knife."

"It's not the Devil's Dagger I want."

I sputtered. "Then why am I here?"

He turned the book in his hands and pointed to an illustration. "Is this what it looks like?"

I cast my eyes down. The page showed a knife with the head of a dragon. While the book depicted the dagger's morphed form, it's not what it looked like now. Right now, the knife was searching for its owner. Which was why the pommel was in the shape of a key.

"Why should I tell you anything?"

Arkenu's lips twitched into a smile. "Soon enough, I'll gain your declaration."

"Of what?" But as soon as I asked I had a realization. "Wait. You? You think you're a descendant of Yair?" He wanted me to recognize him as the forgotten son. "No. Never."

"How can you be so sure?" Arkenu snapped the book closed. "The answer is yes, that is what the Devil's Dagger looks like, but only after its chosen it's wielder. Since it has none, the pommel remains in the shape of a key."

How could he know that? Only a precious few knew that. The dagger hid itself away until a certain time. When the time came for the son to lead all of Neith to safety, a dragon would heed its call. But the only ones who knew about its morphing stage were dragons, drakes, and riders.

Arkenu loomed over me. "This city, the nation, this world is in chaos. There hasn't been a dragon on the throne for thousands of years, and Neith needs a dragon."

He wasn't just talking about Aleenia. He was talking about ruling everything.

"Then find a dragon," I said it like it was so easy. Like one could jaunt over the Ekinphrow sea and join forces with the first beast that flew by. Dragons weren't that easy to find.

"I have found him," Arkenu smirked, proud of his claim.

My apprehension must have shown, because he leaned closer and said, "You will give me that dagger, willingly."

"Even if you have found a dragon, that doesn't prove you to be the forgotten son."

Arkenu shrugged. "He who wins the faith of Yair's descendant shall bequeath the means to transform the disguised to their true form."

The words grated. To hear such divining gibberish made my skin shiver. "I know what the prophecy says." I seethed in anger. Prophecy. What had it ever gotten me but pain. He did not need to cite the prediction to me. I'd combed over the scribble written on the Walls of Insight trying to decipher its meaning for half my life like some fanatical monk.

"Then you know what it means."

I laughed, hearty, long and with exuberance. I'd studied, breathed, and lived prophecy from a young age. Years I'd devoted to deciphering the words on the marble tunnels turned into decades, and the more the time passed, the more those words of prophecy shattered my heart. The years spent trying to find the lost son corrupted my hope. The waiting. The uncertainty. The riddles. The insanity. Never again.

I wiped my eyes. "Only a fool would try to guess what the stones of prophecy mean. They are words the elements cast down to watch mortals fret. Some of them don't make complete sentences. Some are gibberish. They are words slapped together that don't even abide sentence structure."

"You've been to Ekinphrow?" Arkenu's resolute stance remained.

I stopped laughing. Ekinphrow. The place of refugee drakes. Someone had told a human about the city of flight.

About the Stones of Prophecy and the Walls of Insight. "How did you learn about Ekinphrow?"

Arkenu's mouth remained grim. He stood and stared at me with expectation. An answer for an answer, that was the game. I did not want to confirm his question, and in turn, he let go of my pseudo answer and said, "My Pyragon has helped me regain my faith. He's the dragon I need."

"Isn't that backward?"

"Not if I'm the lost son."

This again. "You think the dagger is the 'means bequeathed to reveal the disguised true form'?" I quoted the prophecy, testing his knowledge.

"It only makes sense."

"How?" I wanted to hear him say it. Arkenu knew so many things about dragons. Things only a rider would know. Instinct insisted he was not the rider of the prophecy, but logic was starting to persuade me otherwise.

"The dagger is the key. It will bring forth his true form."

"How?" The answer was obvious to any with God-blood, but gauging how much Arkenu showed me and how much he was reading from me was the real question.

Arkenu, the king of persuasion, paused and assessed me with unrelenting steel eyes. "The dagger is a cutting tool."

He was close. So close to the answer. But this is where Arkenu's knowledge ebbed.

Yes, the dagger was meant to "cut" away at the shell and bring forth a dragon's true form. But if it were not done correctly, it was only good for stabbing.

"I see." The guild master pulled back. "I'll study more on the subject." He went back to his book.

Study. Damnable. He had been reading me. I'd almost been convinced he might be the forgotten son. But "study" wasn't the right word. Riders had memories. Dragon memories. Everything a rider needed to know was found by *pondering*. That's what made them riders. These specific humans were unique from their kind because they shared a bond that carried down from dam to child. Arkenu would not need to research anything. Damnable deep Waters. Even his so-called dragon might have told him as much. And there it was. The answer. I had to find out if the rumors were true. If Arkenu had a dragon in his guild, and if that was where the assassin was getting his information.

"I wish to meet your dragon." I cringed knowing everything the Aegis predicted was coming true.

Arkenu shifted his gaze to me.

I cleared my throat. "It would help me determine if the dagger is truly yours."

Not that I didn't have his full attention before, but now the light in his eyes shone with opportunity. A tiny smirk lifted the right side of his lips. He took his time answering me. "I was wondering when you would ask."

"Alone."

He lifted his eyebrow, his gaze penetrating my motive. "No."

"What could I do to a dragon? If he's loyal, you have no reason to pause."

"My word is final."

"If you have a dragon, they will speak the truth." And the possible source of Arkenu's knowledge.

He smirked and went back to reading.

"What?" I scoffed.

"Truth is often a prophet's guide."

I grabbed the nearest book in my reach and flipped through the pages, pretending to scan words. He was maddening. I was beginning to think he got his way by driving his opponents insane, twisting their minds until they saw the world his way. But how he saw the world and how he wanted to fix it... well, only a madman would consider a prophecy, a knife, and a dragon the solutions to save a doomed world.

CHAPTER 7

ZEROH

Kuval set the bucket down, leaned back on the table, and considered me. "No."

I raised my head to look at him. "What, are you judge, jury, and executioner?"

"Death is the easy way out. You're not getting the easy way."

"Wonderful. No out for me."

Kuval stared at the ground, no doubt in reflection. The carefreeness had been wiped from his demeanor. He snapped out of his thoughts, straightened, and sat next to me. He was within burning distance with our hips touching.

"Tell me his name." Kuval laid a hand on my stomach. Despite all he'd done, his touch calmed the fluttering of angry bees inside. I hated myself for it.

"Why? So, you can suss out all the gory details?"

"You've been holding onto this for six years, right? That can't be good."

I turned my head away. For several moments, all that connected us was his hand on my skin and our hips touching. This was worse than two elements fighting to get to each other through me.

Kuval made lazy circles around my navel. He looked at my midsection as he spoke. "I don't remember much about my mother. She took off when I was young."

My eyes looked up into his thoughtful face.

"You might think I'd hate her for that, but I don't. I'm glad she got out. As for my father. . . well, he was a drunk that liked to fight his son and prove he was still *the* man."

He cast a smile at me. "I tell you this not for a tit for tat but because I want you to understand you're not alone. You don't have to be all alone."

Burn it all. Maybe it was his touch, or his sincerity. Perhaps, his open expression or maybe all of it that made me strong enough to be vulnerable.

"Va. . ." My voice choked up, and I cleared my throat. "Vavar." My eyes stung and I stared up at the ceiling. "He was fun. Lively. I might have. . . stayed with him. He. . . um. . . we were exploring. The kind when kids are horny. He went down. . . on me. I. . . I think there was a split second when he. . . he. . . felt pain, maybe. Then. . . cinders."

I closed my eyes. Judgment from Kuval, of all people, would shatter me. That's all I ever received. People's eyes accused me of crimes they built in their heads. Part of me didn't blame them. The truth was worse than their imaginations.

Kuval wiped a thumb over my wet cheek. "Damn. Dragon tears. Eldyn would kill me for letting them fall like this."

Lips pressed to mine. Thoughtless, I opened my mouth and let his tongue sweep me away. He tasted of prime meat and juices. My cock twitched and came alive. I ripped my head away. "Wait."

"All that you've been taught has gone against your instincts. You don't actually hate this, do you?"

I couldn't look him in the eye. "No."

"Does it feel wrong?"

"No. Just inappropriate."

Kuval laughed. "Inappropriate—I've been called worse."

"So have I." A smile ghosted over my face.

For a moment, Kuval sat by my side, gazing at me, pushing his fingers over the mess of saliva and olive oil still clinging to my skin with a tenacity to admire.

"Are you going to collect the bounty on my head?"

"No." Kuval shook his head.

"That just frightens me more."

He grinned. "I do plan on finishing what I started." Kuval stepped off the altar and leaned over my stomach.

"Why?" I threw a look of disbelief.

"Well, one, because the thought of watching you explode after a six-year hiatus is too tempting." He bent down and sucked the last pool of juices trapped in my navel. His tongue rolled inside my concave belly button. A lightning-strike sensation flashed through my middle and down to my balls.

Shhhiiiit. I pulled on my bonds. My cock bobbed to life. I squirmed not knowing if I should like this, fight it, or both. At least, my guilt was still intact, but it wasn't communicating to my lower half. My breathing hitched, and I turned my head to the side, trying to escape from absorbing the intense attack. "What's the other reason?"

He leaned up, letting me catch my breath.

"Two, it's valuable." He fetched a vial from the case. "Three, there are others that are in need of it."

"Valuable?" I huffed. "Seriously?"

Kuval didn't expand on his answers. "Let me set you free."

"By all means." I rattled the wrist and ankle clamps.

He threw his head back and laughed. "Then I'll teach you to fly in bondage."

"That's not going to work." The pressure of hormones was a ferocious hunger. In the past, despite the risk and shame, I'd tried spilling into water, containers, and even campfires to try and counteract the aftermath of my orgasm. "I've tried a few things. Nothing works."

"Now you're just admitting to other blazes."

I had no defense. He was right. The fires I started had done damage. All two containers I had used, one metal and one bone, held for thirty seconds before they had blasted apart. And other fire—well that was a complete disaster. I might have well asked a thief to hold all my gold. Water had doused those other fires, and I made sure they had been out, but I had paid for it. The bodily relief wasn't worth the aftermath.

Kuval caressed my abs with his tongue. My body squirmed with pleasure. I flexed seeking out more. Guilt crushed me. I shouldn't give in. But maybe he was right, and the vial was magic. Or maybe this was a death sentence.

I could deal with my death. But I couldn't handle killing even one more person from my dirty lust.

"Please. . . wait. Listen to me." I tried avoiding the gentle nips of his teeth along my hip.

"Has it really been that long?" He swirled his tongue over my thigh.

I shivered. "Five years, six months, and ten days."

Kuval moved up and lay next to me. He set his hand on my cock as if it were a perfect coaster for his palm. "Kid, you need to let go. Everything your foster parents told you was a lie."

"They didn't lie." They were also the only parents I'd ever known. I didn't consider anything foster about them.

"Did they teach you that you were normal? That love comes in a perfectly prepared box? That you can only have one type of sex?" He slid his thumb over the tip of my cock.

I didn't answer. Couldn't really. All sensation pulsed waves of pleasure from my nether regions.

"Of course they did." Kuval continued his assault. "Because they don't understand that there are no boundaries, of any sort, with dragons."

Sighing, I shut my lip and didn't argue. "Whatever," I managed to squeak out.

"Zeroh, you've said wait, you've said hold on, you've even said stop, but you've yet to say no."

I turned my face to him, cleared my throat, and said, "All right then. No."

"Fine," Kuval huffed and got up.

He set the vial back in the box and closed the lid. Then he stepped on the altar near my shoulder and fiddled with the water contraption above my head, hooking the lip of the neck to a clasp connected to the ceiling. He stepped down and walked to the door. When he turned the sprocket, water rushed through the pipes.

Oh, *fúrr*. "Kuval?"

"I'm going out." He faced the door as he spoke. "I need to clear my head."

"Kuval. . . wait. Um. . . I change my mind. Go ahead, have sex with me all you want."

He shook his head. "Your 'no' was resolute. I'm not someone that begs or forces himself on others."

"Okay, I'll beg. Have sex with me." I tried for funny, but Kuval didn't laugh. He looked haggard, dejected, and lonely.

But I had bigger problems. Pain. Lots of it. Water would come for me, and I wasn't ready for another bout of splash tackle. But the underlying problem was I did want his touch.

Why had I waited two days to kill him? If I were truthful, I couldn't do it that first day. Or the second. Even on the third night, I was making excuses to postpone his death.

He cast a look at the barrel of water. "Doa o ki ni." Then he turned the sprocket again and slipped out into the night.

"Kuval! Kuval! Please! At least, tell me when you're coming back, you bastard!"

I looked up at the water contraption. Oh, *fúrr*. Oh, *fúrr*. Oh, *fúrr*. The tiniest of water drops peeked over the lip. Even though Water had no mouth, I swear it grinned at me.

CHAPTER 8

ELDYN

"I'm beginning to think this dragon is an exaggeration at best." Spending a night on a desk with not so much as a bucket to piss in proved more torturous than I previously thought. I'd finally been given a place to relieve myself, and water to drink, but food had been lacking.

"I don't pretend to command him. I ask. He grants." Arkenu left me overnight returning in the wee hours of the morning with nothing but a book in his hands. "If you're that anxious to meet him, then claim me my right. You'll see plenty of him then."

Though I was hungry, I wasn't that desperate. Well, I was starving, but I wasn't beyond caring. I remained cognizant enough to hear the threat in his words. A warning involving all of Aleenia.

"You're not the forgotten son."

Arkenu flashed his eyes in irritation. That part of the prophecy that garnished "bequeath the means" was the only thing saving my butt. If the prophecy said *take the means*, I'm sure Arkenu would have interpreted that as kill the person who has the knife and claim it for your own. It was a good thing he took prophecy seriously. But then again, if his method was to drive me mad with his own brand of logic, this would be a torturous road. I might end up giving him the knife to keep my sanity.

He acquired the only chair in the room while I carefully shifted through the bookshelf. I'd determined his knowledge of drakes came from books. But books gave a fraction of the story. Arkenu was an intelligent man and a talented researcher. He'd cobbled passages and made sense of them, put them together in a way to make me question my instincts. But he would have to do better than cite forgotten lore in tomes too old for reprinting.

Soon as Arkenu sat down, he began his onslaught to prove himself worthy of the Devil's Dagger and, by extension, the rightful ruler of Neith. "Humans don't have magic, but riders do."

Reaching for a book, my hand paused. I almost corrected him. Human riders shared their dragon's magic after they bonded. If the rider were a drake, they inherited their own magic.

"It won't work," I whispered.

"You have so much knowledge to share."

"Not with you." I pulled out the book I wanted and started reading.

As his dark eyes settled on me, a shiver ran down my spine. My life dangled by the width of a spider web. I dared not call upon Water because there was still the slightest wedge of doubt that Arkenu could feel my elemental rise. Still Waters ran deep though, and I was upset, which meant, sooner or later, Water would try to comfort me.

A gusty breeze tossed a maple leaf through the window.

Arkenu flinched. The wind of a metallic blur brushed my long blue-white locks aside. He'd thrown something too fast for me to see.

He remained with his hand outstretched, intense eyes fixed on whatever it was behind me. His focus made me turn to see what had set off the assassin.

Behind me, stabbed through and hanging to the stone wall by a throwing knife, was the maple leaf that had flown in with the draft.

"Paranoid often?" I sniggered, partially from nerves. The man was silent death.

"Your second element, it's Ether."

Blood ran from my face. "That wasn't me."

Yes, I commanded Wind. It used to be my primary element. But after my dreams. . . dreams of my dragon, I'd changed immediately to Hydra. I'd studied Water like nothing else. Burrowed deep into the ways of Water. When the element of Water came easy to me, it bolstered my path. I'd abandoned Wind. Yet Ether never abandoned me.

Arkenu shifted over to the knife and pulled his dagger from the wall, taking the maple leaf and tossing it out the window.

I snarled and angrily turned to hide my seething animosity. Ether was only bringing me a gift, and he'd tossed it like some week-old bread crust. I shoved my hands inside the sleeves of my robes and grasped the Devil's Dagger. How I wanted to let him have the pointed side of the knife.

I squared my shoulders and relaxed my hold. Now was not the time.

CHAPTER 9

ZEROH

TIME HAD NO MEANING. There was only eternity and then pain. The powerful blow of the second droplet hit me square in the chest and knocked the wind out of my lungs. I had no measurement to tell how far apart the droplets fell. The time between them spanned forever.

"Kuval!" *Please come back. I changed my mind. Please come back.*

My prayer was answered. The door opened. Kuval slumped in the doorway. He gripped a brown paper bag in his right hand. The open lip of a liquor bottle peeked from the top of the sack. His other hand helped steady himself against the door frame. He mumbled something, turned the water off, and shut the door behind him.

Drunk bastard.

Kuval set the bottle and paper bag down and picked up a towel. He shuffled over to me. A forlorn expression on his handsome face. He sat down and pressed the towel against my chest.

I clenched my teeth against the burning sensation. Then relief. He'd soaked what little Water lay on my chest into the towel. His glazed-over eyes scanned me, lingering on my bare middle.

"It was love at first sight, ya know," he said, his words slurred, hinting at his drunken state. He wasn't as sharp as I'd seen him before. "Stupid dragon."

I kept my mouth shut. My protesting about being a dragon would make him "wrong." Finding out how the thief dealt with conflict in his current mental space was not wise.

"You walked in and then splat." He threw an arm out, tossing the towel aside. "My heart against the wall." He stood up and shuffled to the door again.

No. He was leaving? I couldn't take any more Water torture. Anything was better than being pounded, burned, and ripped apart.

Swallowing my pride, I croaked, "Touch me."

Kuval stopped in mid-shuffle. He didn't turn. Didn't look back. Didn't answer. He just stood there.

My heart raced. Please don't go. I forced myself to swallow the sandstorm coating my mouth.

He changed course and walked to the paper bag. "Do you like chocolate?"

"Chocolate?" Had he heard my offer?

"Greta makes the best brownies."

I heard the crinkle of paper, then Kuval turned around. He held a chocolate-frosted brownie in one hand and the liquor bottle in the other. His eyes, while still glazed over, twinkled in mirth.

"How did you get something like that at this time of night?" I was trying to gauge how long I'd been here. If I had to guess, it had to be the wee early buds of morning. People weren't awake at this hour. There were no shops open. In fact, he'd probably been kicked out of whatever bar he'd gotten the liquor from. . . unless. "Thief!"

"I paid for it." He shambled over.

"Meaning you broke into the shop and left money on the counter." I lifted my chin.

He blinked. "See, you do it too."

"That's still stealing." At least, I didn't lie to myself about that.

"Greta's fine with it." He sat down next to me. "Hope you like male brownies."

"Male?"

"It has nuts in it." Kuval shoved the brownie in my mouth.

I took a bite and chewed. Oh, *fürr*. The delectable treat had enough chocolate to stave off a serious craving. If chocolate was his thing, this would cure a sweet tooth for a week. The soft, buttery morsel melted until I tasted walnuts. I moaned in appreciation. This was better than getting hammered by Water. Anything else was preferable to getting slammed by an angry element.

Kuval took the other half of the brownie and popped it into his mouth. He opened the bottle and took a swig of alcohol. Then, he tipped the lip of the bottle over my mouth.

"Open."

I did. He poured the liquid into my mouth as he would if it were a cup.

The burn of single malt Scotch scorched my senses, flashed down my gullet, and cleared my mind.

"Trying to get me drunk?"

He chewed. looking over my naked body. It was a unique experience to be eye fondled. My cheeks warmed. The thrill of his touch made it clear—when push came to shove, I enjoyed pleasure.

"So, are we doing this?" My anxiety took the better hold of my mouth.

"Doing what?"

Shit. Please don't leave. Please don't turn on that contraption again. "Fucking."

"What changed your mind?"

"Does it matter?"

"Yes." His head bobbed.

Collecting my thoughts, I started with the main reason. "I realized that I can't go on like this forever. I like being touched. One day, I'm going to try again with some hairbrained scheme. I might think a snowy mountain range would be enough to contain my. . . umm. . ."

"Spunk?" Kuval supplied.

"You're so crude."

He shrugged.

"It's just if this vialed Ether works, great. If it doesn't, I'll pay the price."

"Does the water pipe have anything to do with your decision?"

That gave me pause. "I'll admit I want the pain to stop. But if I'm going to die here. . ."

"No!" Kuval sat on the ground near the altar. "I promise you that. You won't die. Not by my hand."

"It's fine. I've made peace with it. If this doesn't work, I'll die as soon as that vial explodes and burns the roof down anyway. You said yourself you'd be fine."

He smirked. "And if it doesn't explode? Will you be able to live with yourself afterward?"

I snorted. "Bring it. I could do worse."

Kuval laughed. "Well, thanks for the compliment."

For the first time, I looked upon Kuval without the tint of his titles. Thief. Assassin. Torturer. He was a man. A fine-looking one too. A lover I could claim without shame. I tasted the thought. Lover. Yes, I dare say I could do much worse than Kuval. It did not mean I wouldn't kill him as soon as I were free though.

His eyes glazed over as if he were in a dream. That expression—I'd seen it on other people. I'd seen it on pickpockets staring at a gold piece lying in the middle of the street, on cooks waiting for their pie to cool, between lovers entwined. Lust. I'd seen it, but being the object of such desire? Not since Vavar.

No. Glares reserved for me were ones of disdain, disgust, revulsion, indifference, contempt, ridicule. I endured all of them. I deserved them. But this. . . this expression crippled me sure as if my legs were taken away. Even if my limbs were free, I'd be paralyzed by his glossy-eyed open desire. How this thief could cut my heart so deep remained a mystery.

Within his expression of desire was a world of acceptance, affection, fondness, and passion. But it was the respect within that world that stole my breath. I had plummeted down a pit. I'd never recover from this. I wasn't sure I wanted to climb out. Nor did I think I'd be strong enough to name that pit. Or recognize it, much less admit its name.

My body unclenched, and I looked away. His admiration chilled my resolve to remain detached. I turned my head, unable to accept this strange new yearning. That look couldn't possibly be reserved for me. I was a fool to think he was thinking of me. He must be thinking of someone else.

His hand pinched my chin and pulled my face to his. "Look at me."

With his permission, I did. His expression softened. Whatever he'd found in my eyes pleased him.

"Don't be afraid of me. Don't be afraid of. . . my love."

My eyes widened. Love? Why wouldn't I be afraid of Kuval? Even if I was prepared, he was a force of nature. I was just a magic trick.

"Don't throw that word at me." I wrenched my head out of his grip.

"You think you don't deserve love?"

"I know I don't."

"You didn't kill him on purpose."

I clenched my teeth and growled. "You don't get to throw that in my face."

"My apologies. I won't bring it up again."

This torture was worse. He would destroy me by continuing this kindness, the restraint he showed me at every bend. He had several chances to kill me and hadn't. He could have left me to die by Water. He hadn't. He had fed me. Soothed me with his gentleness. I'd burned his hands, tried to kill him, and here he was tempting me with chocolate, feeding me, telling me I mattered, arguing with me like a friend. If he continued, he'd leave me thinking I was worth having.

Then what? When Arkenu found me, or if I escaped, or Kuval let me go. . . I'd be left as a shell. Only good enough as a cooking fire. I imagined my sorrow would keep my Fire burning till the day I died. But my *Fúrr* would burn in slow, listless hopelessness.

"You will destroy me."

"I will empower you." He laid a palm on my stomach, stilling the roiling inside.

"So, how does this work?" I tried to come off as nonchalant. My voice didn't cooperate. I expected him to laugh. He didn't.

"Are you trying to take advantage of a drunk guy?"

With a sputter, I said, "I'm the one in chains."

"So, it's okay if the drunk guy is trying to take advantage of you?"

A groan slipped from my lips. "Ugh, do what you want. You obviously do, whether you're knackered or not."

He skimmed a palm over my side while keeping the one hand on my middle firmly in place. "Hands first then."

It was as if he were holding me steady, even though my ankles and wrists were locked against the altar. His touch helped calm my nerves.

His roaming hand covered my entire chest. From fingers to wrist, his touch enveloped me—literally. The length of his fingers wrapped around my waist. "Now that it's come to my attention that this body has been neglected, I'm going to show you pleasure as often as possible."

"I don't want that." My back arched into his warmth.

"Yes, you do. Everyone wants love. Even dragons." His hand went up and over my neck.

"I wish you'd stop calling me that." My reaction to him was strong. I lifted my chin and exposed my throat.

His thumb washed over my Adam's apple. "Dragons love with their whole being."

My cock twitched and thumped on top of his other hand. I suppressed a moan.

"Fire dragons love down to their essence."

"And chocolate-thieving assassins? Do they love?"

He smiled down at me as if I'd said something clever. "When I'm done, you'll sing how much you desire my cock."

A cool liquid slid down my balls. Kuval poured olive oil all over my lower region and slicked up my cock. I burst out in moans. Losing myself. I feared becoming a slave to his rhythm. He squeezed going down and let go pulling up. My undisciplined hips started meeting his down stroke.

"Very nice." Kuval leaned down. He opened his mouth, and powerless to stop, I watched him suckle my rod. The monster I'd been holding back sprang lose inside my gut.

"Kuval. . ." My body convulsed. Every nerve came alive. All the hairs on my arms rose. My eyes fluttered. His fingers rimmed my taboo hole. The sensation propelled me towards an endless hunger.

"Yes," I breathed.

He pushed until my ass swallowed his digit. He was inside. Connected. How wonderful—letting someone give me this, letting Kuval, the force of nature, give me pleasure. My cock stiffened and waggled in the air. I'd been hard in the past and calmed down in time before any spunk shot out. But now, there was no way. My orgasm started building.

"Kuval, wait. . ." I cracked open my eyes. "Let me calm down."

His eyes glowed with intense fascination. "Relax. I've got you."

"Kuval—"

"Trust me." He smoothed a hand over my chest. Electric lightning shot through my brain. Sensation overrode logic. I was a mess of passion and greed. Those hands threw me into orbit. Then his lips, pressing against my neck, grounded me.

I moaned, delirious with pleasure. I tried telling my uncontrollable cock to stand down. To not get excited. But this incredible current running up and down my body wouldn't let up. Nor did I have the willpower to withstand Kuval's touch. I wanted more.

His hands wavered over my chest, down to my core. The tremble in my stomach encouraged me to release everything.

"Please. . ." But I was careful in my asking. If I told him to stop, he would.

"What do you want?" The tips of his fingers skimmed my nipples.

"Ungggh. . ." My mind went blank. My cock bobbed. "Please. . ." I raised my head and prayed to *fúrr*. He understood. "Just touching." My heart tried scaling the ladder of my ribs and escaping. "I can't take much more." I'd explode if he continued.

"Baby, trust me."

I shook my head. "You'll die."

Kuval smirked and thumbed my lower lip. "So, you're not worried about the Water overhead crashing down on you?"

Water? Where? What Water? "Of course, that too."

"But that's not going to happen. I'll temper that love lava for you."

Sheesh, he was so cheesy. "Glass isn't going to hold it."

Kuval straddled me, held my face in his gentle, firm grasp, and didn't let me escape into myself. "I know what I'm doing."

The cadence of my panting measured moments. "And what will you do with me once I've given in?"

He stroked my chest like a familiar pet. "What would you do if I let you go?"

Hardening my heart, I remembered who I was, what I was, and said, "Finish my job." I still owed Arkenu. Still belonged to the Kenwald guild. But I wasn't sure I could go through with my goal. Not after this.

Kuval leaned down until his chest was on mine. His breath tickled my ear. He smelled like chocolate and Scotch. "Then you'll be strung up with me for a very long time."

He wasn't going to kill me. The thief had other plans. While the thought both terrified me and confused me, a certain part of me started warming to the idea of a companion. *Stop it, Zeroh. Don't let him suck you in.*

"I can see the question on your face." Kuval sat up and smiled down at me. "If I wanted to kill you, I'd hand you over to the bounty." He leaned down again, stroking my arms as he went. "You're not the only one needing release." He rolled his hips. The impressive bulge in his pants didn't disgust me like I thought it might. He was turned on. The lust in his eyes melted my resolve to remain celibate.

I swallowed the lump in my throat. "I'm terrified."

The haze of want cleared from his eyes and the glow of compassion shone through.

"Zeroh, I've got you." His hand cupped the side of my face. "I promise. You'll have nothing but pleasure."

My heart thudded hard. "But—"

"Zeroh, do you think I want to die?"

"I believe you think a six-inch knuckle-width glass vial will hold a volcano."

He smirked and slid his hand down over my chest. "And you don't trust me?"

"You're a thief!"

"Is that a no?" He skimmed his fingers down along my ribs, then over my hip and toward the inside of my thigh.

I jolted at his touch, raising my chest. At the same time, I wanted to lean into this touch, but also wanted to escape from the intensity. His other hand settled on my stomach, anchoring me once more.

"I'll prove this vial can hold a volcano then."

"Do I have a choice?"

He hummed an amused sound, telling me no way. Kuval leaned down and planted soft lips against my chest. "You have a choice. You can say no."

I fought against the soothing touch, arching, and twisting. As he inched down, leaving tiny devastating, lush kisses, anticipation built in my nether regions. I wanted to let go. All the crap from my past ate at my soul.

"How long do you expect to last?" He looked up from under his long eyelashes.

"I won't cum."

His muffled laugh swept warm breath over my right hip, making me fight my chains. He ran his nose along my abdomen, grazing my cock. I heaved a breath and arched my back. Oh, *furr*. So good. My mind went blank. My sight went black. I moaned. The sound was not little or low.

"You were saying?"

I panted. "I won't cum."

"Oh, a challenge." His eyes widened. The dancing mirth in his face sent my confidence in a nose dive. But I'd had years of training in ejaculation control. Better known as orgasm denial.

"Have you withheld all this time?" Kuval circled his fingers over my hips.

"Yes." I gritted my teeth and bucked.

The lust in Kuval's eyes returned. "Then I'd say you're ready to pop."

His hand width spanned my entire waist. With that advantage, he used both palms to massage my front. His fingers electrified me, sending me to heights I didn't dare cross before. His eyes promised tantalizing mystery. The tattoos on his shoulders and arms mesmerized me.

Unable to look away, I followed the roll of his muscles. If he did nothing more than touch my skin-starved body, I'd ache for weeks. I could come from just this. Kuval's hands sent me floating, but at the same time his strong hands, pinning my middle, anchored me. I was free yet secure. A kite held by string allowed to wander in a sky of pleasure. I would get lost in the clouds, but always have a connection to home. He stroked my body sending that string out into the heavens, then kissed my chest, pulling the string in towards an earthly base.

I shut my eyes and strained to keep inappropriate gasps to myself. The more he stroked the more desensitized and relaxed I became. The more I let myself be sotted in ecstasy.

Those strong hands held me firm under his spell. His fingers were as precise as his skill with a knife, brushing along my skin. Every touch cut into me. Magic hands grazed over my neck further and further up every pass. Every round, I lifted my chin a fraction, exposing my throat.

"I've got you," he whispered. Slowly, Kuval wrapped his palm over my throat and put enough pressure on my neck to make me believe he was in control. "I've got you."

A whimper escaped my lips, and I opened into his hold. Chin to the ceiling, eyes closed, all my muscles went taut and melted at the same time. I let Kuval wrap me in a cocoon of safety.

"I've got you."

For that brief moment, Kuval was responsible for me. I was free of petty choices. Unburdened. Holding back was no longer necessary.

"I've got you."

His hand slipped back down leaving me in this euphoric bliss. The ends of my lips curled into a slight smile. I looked through a half-lidded gaze.

Kuval sucked in a breath. "Fucking gorgeous." Lust burned in his eyes. "You like being held don't you."

I wiggled my hips in the guise of getting comfortable.

"You have no shame by being mastered by me."

His strong hands gave me strength. Strength enough to admit the truth. I felt safe. Kuval was a thief and an assassin, but there was no better person to understand someone like me.

"What do you think?" I said.

He chuckled. "Don't want to admit to anything, do you? That's okay. Your body tells me the truth." To prove his point, he smoothed his hands over my hard cock.

Proud that I didn't jolt at his handling, I nonetheless enjoyed every inch of his masculine fingers roaming my skin.

"That was fast."

"Fast?" I looked up.

"I thought you'd fight the pleasure till the end."

My lips curled upward. "Oh, you'll have a fight. Just because I'm enjoying this doesn't mean I'm going to spurt ropes."

He raked his nails down my sides.

"Fuck!" I jolted at his brutal tactic. My cock bobbed and stretched for maximum length. Pre-cum spilled onto my stomach.

Kuval gave a measured look to my drooling eye. His finger hovered over my weeping head. He was hesitant. He should be afraid.

"I thought you were experienced in Pyromages."

He flicked his eyes to me. "I am. That's why I'm being cautious."

My weeping head drooled. For whatever illogical reason, my pre-cum wasn't flammable. Knowing Kuval was safe from the clear liquid oozing down from my cock, I couldn't help but tease him. "Afraid to touch it? Have you gained your sanity?"

"Sometimes, a pairing isn't compatible, and the couple has. . . issues."

"Issues as in, the pre-cum burns the partner?" I smirked.

He narrowed his eyes and poked at my drooling head. He looked at his finger and tested the consistency with his thumb and forefinger. Nothing, as I expected. But Kuval smiled in triumph.

"Yeah, yeah." I set my head down.

He stuck the pre-cum finger in his mouth and closed his eyes. His expression turned reverent. Damn. I couldn't stay mad at him. Not with him worshipping my cock.

Kuval bent down and licked the spot where my drooling snake spilled its poison.

"Kuval!" I yelped in surprise. "The *furr*. That's enough."

He smacked his lips with a sheepish smile. "You taste like mint."

"Do you not understand that's like drinking kerosene!"

He shrugged. "So, don't light up."

I moaned in frustration. "Idiot!"

Then my cock was encased in wet and suction. My mind froze. Oh, that felt so good. My hips automatically pumped. Tension started building in my balls. My eyes fluttered. But as much as I loved him sucking my cock, I would neither let him die nor keep going. I pulled at my chained wrists.

"Kuval, please don't do that."

Our eyes met. He pulled up and let my cock out of his mouth. A hand cupped my face.

"All right. You don't have to cry about it."

"I'm not crying."

His thumb swept along my cheek and a cool wetness streaked my face. "I promise you're not in danger."

"I'm not worried about me." Fuck. That came out wrong. "I mean, I don't care about you, or rather, that you die. The way you die—that's what I care about."

He chuckled in his wise, sage, knowing way. So annoying.

"So, you're telling me I'm good enough to break your self-induced dry spell."

"You know what, just fucking do whatever." I dropped my head.

"I'm honored." He grabbed the bottle and poured olive oil in his hand. Then with his slicked up palm, he grabbed my cock and started pumping.

My whole body wanted to clench around that single most sensitive spot. But the chains around my ankles and wrists prevented me from going far.

Breaths came in panting waves. His caress was gentle, yet firm, and applied the perfect amount of pressure to drive me mindless. For a long moment, I indulged in the luxury of Kuval's touch. His hand slammed down at the base of my cock enough to make me convulse. I snapped my hips and dived into oblivion. Shivers rolled up my spine and hit a part of my brain that made the rest of my body unable to resist. But I had to fight. My orgasm waited under my satisfying shudders.

His hand hit me in the right spots. His down stroke felt so good. It was like I was slamming home. Oh, *furr*. If he stopped now, I'd have blue balls for life. But if I didn't stop now, I'd cum, thus sending the equivalent of a volcano out into the world. This tower would burn. This town would be ashes. Everyone would die. And it would be my fault. I had to hold on until he was tired or bored of his plaything.

"I've got you, baby." He set his other hand on my chest.

Right when my resistance built, he spoke. His words assaulted my common sense. I was too busy shivering under his touch to answer or give him a snide comment.

"You're gorgeous." His eyes roamed over me. "I don't think I'll get enough of you anytime soon."

"Kuval, I—too much. . . I can't hold back. I'll, I'll cum."

His hand on my chest rubbed up and down. "I know, baby. I just needed to get you acclimated, or you're gonna black out when I use the vial. I want to make sure you're awake for the finale."

Oil poured over the tip of my cock. The stream of liquid slid down my shaft leaving trails of cool wetness behind. The oil spilled over my balls, pooled at the base of my cock, and overflowed between my thighs.

Kuval fondled my sack, gently rubbing the oil in my skin like lotion.

"Relax, baby."

"That's not going to make me relax."

"Tell me if you get uncomfortable."

"What? Why?"

He hooked his thumb under my balls. A finger rimmed my puckered hole. It was wet.

Kuval gasped.

"Don't put so much oil in me." My grumble of a protest died when his supreme smile cast down on me.

"Well, well. Looks like we won't be needing any lubricant."

A finger pushed at my hole. . . and went in easily as if I'd invited him. He was pushing in and out of me. It was as though his whole hand was coated in cream. "You don't need oil." His bedroom eyes sparkled.

I lifted my head and asked, "Is that not normal?" I'd frown but it was so good.

"Dragons have different anatomy than humans," he purred.

I huffed and laid my head back down. That again.

"You don't need oil. You produce your own slick here." He pulled his finger out and breeched my outer rim once more.

My insides clenched at the sensation. I flexed, trying to move but the chains held me down.

"Feel that?" He pushed his finger in further.

"It feels strange."

"Because it's your first time." He smoothed his other hand over my chest. Kuval easily slid a finger up my back channel, and as promised it didn't hurt. There was pressure, but no pain.

"Give me a second to reach your spot." He grabbed my cock and balls again and started slowly pumping me. His fingers did the same, using my natural lubricant to invade my insides. My ass was being stretched and worked over. The scent of sex intoxicating.

"Despite your complaints, your body is accepting me like an old lover." Kuval pushed inside me, testing my limitations. He'd also rubbed a part of me that made my breath hitch.

He grinned. "There it is."

"There is what?" I gasped.

"Your spot." He flexed his finger and brushed against that spot again. This time my stomach dropped and left me breathless.

Our eyes locked and I knew. The fight over my orgasm was done. "Kuval. . ."

"I've got you, Zeroh. Let go."

My heart sank and my face crumpled. "You're making a mistake." I'd kill everyone including myself. My orgasm was ready to burst forth. Violently.

Kuval reached over to the box and grabbed a vial. "Don't worry, I know what I'm doing."

I closed my eyes. "Famous last words."

Then, the head of my cock was encased. There were no words to describe the sensation. I was being sucked into the vial with such force my body went on sensory overload.

"Holy, *fúrr!*"

"I know." Kuval smiled. "Rather intense."

Now I understood what he meant by preparing me. This wasn't like anything I'd ever experienced. Sure, I remembered the brief moment of pleasure when Vavar got on his knees and sent my troubles packing. But this. . . this was a never-ending, no release, nonstop suction that bordered on painful.

I started convulsing. Every part of my body clutched in preparation for the onslaught. My hands balled into fists. My toes curled. My back arched. A shudder ripped through me. My mind went utterly still. I was cumming. I threw my head back as the first stream shot into the vial. I screamed in mindless pleasure. My cock pumped another shot, and another, and another. I called out through each thick spurt. And I kept cumming.

The glass held. But I had no space in my head to marvel at the miracle. My orgasm persisted as if it would never cease. My pleasured cries chased out coherent words. I twisted in this half-arched, half-paralyzed contortion. As the vial filled, I realized the ropes of cum were not stopping any time soon.

"See, I knew you needed this," Kuval muttered.

Voiceless and with my limbs clamped down, all I could do was watch knowing my semen would overflow the vial.

"Ahhh. . . Zeroh?" Kuval must have come to the same conclusion.

"Shit!" Kuval acted fast. He stretched out and grabbed another vial. He pulled the cork of the empty vial with his teeth and waited, while I remained helpless through an endless orgasm, Kuval traded containers between spurts. The second vial covered my cock head just before my lava cum touched air.

With a perfect transfer between vials and not a drop spilled, Kuval smiled in triumph.

I laid my head down and cried out from the intense, racking tremors throughout my body. My orgasm was still going. Fuck. This was insane. When would it end?

"Crap, kid." Kuval was stretching for another vial. My vision darkened. My throat ran dry. Convulsions racked my body. This orgasm was going to drain me of every last drop.

Kuval did another vial exchange, and finally, finally, this never-ending orgasm slowed. After three-quarters of the third vial was filled, I had nothing left to give.

"I'd say you've been sufficiently drained." Kuval capped the last vial and placed it with the others in the box.

My limbs lay heavy against the marble slab at my back. Yet my soul floated on a cloud. Satisfied. For the first time since I'd burned down my hometown, I was ready for sleep. Real sleep. The restful kind with no nightmares.

Unconsciousness pulled me down a rabbit hole. A melodic song called out from the pit of my soul, drifting into my ears, and then everything faded to black.

CHAPTER 10

ELDYN

EARLY MORNING TURNED INTO early evening. Hunger became the focus to my actions and Arkenu was trying to take advantage of my distracted state. But I was privy to his methods. He was trying to get me to reveal more about drakes, riders, and the Devil's Dagger.

"There's a question I've been asking myself." Arkenu sat in the chair he'd moved over next to the door. "Maybe you can help me answer it."

"What's the saying? You can always ask." I kept vigil by the bookshelf. It was defiance on my part that I did not sit when the Aegis was with me. The small measure of control helped keep my defenses up.

Arkenu dipped a hand into his cloak and pulled out my favorite fruit. A golden pear. There were no such things as coincidences. If there looked to be one, it meant I was not looking at the whole picture or there was information I didn't have. So, I didn't believe he just happened to have a pear because he was hungry. No. The guild master had a method to his subtle torture.

Damnable. I would not falter like this. I would not give up information for something as weak as food.

Arkenu shined the pear, rubbing it against his velvet cloak. "I've been wondering, why does a drake come into human territory, set up shop, and live away from his own kind?"

He bit into the soft skin of the golden pear. The fruit, not as crisp as an apple, didn't make snapping noises, but it wasn't supposed to. A golden pear was perfectly ripe when the skin was soft. As Arkenu's teeth sank into the fruit, I imagined the pear at its peak ripeness, and my mouth watered. He chewed and swallowed.

I kept the drool from slipping out of my mouth.

"Spying perhaps?"

"No." My answer immediate.

Arkenu narrowed his eyes and took another bite of pear and smacking his lips before swallowing.

Saliva pooled at the back of my throat.

"You came from the east, on a boat no other had seen before. Despite the unusual ship, the superior craftsmanship did not go unnoticed."

Where I came from, boats needed to handle rough seas, storms, and hurricanes. Dragons used to fly us over the great waters, but since the days of Casflamir's War, no dragon was willing to sail, fly, or swim to this side of the divide. Not anymore. Over the age, we'd developed ships that rode the ocean like a Hydragon.

"Your element is Water. Not surprising if you came from a seafaring tribe. But you're here for a reason."

I shrugged. "Everyone is here for a reason."

"This city is the seat of Neith. Rule Aleenia. Unite the world."

"Sounds like your reason isn't overly presumptuous." I snorted after my sarcastic comment.

Arkenu took a knife out and cut into an uneaten part of the pear. "Are you looking for an object? One that perhaps you found. And since you found it, you have no more loyalty to the people around you?" He ate the sliver of fruit he'd cut.

I swallowed air. Didn't answer. Let him think what he wanted.

"Perhaps, you're searching for your horde?"

My lip curled into a snarl, and I growled a dragon's warning. "What do you know about it?"

"Peace, elder. I meant no harm." He cut another chunk of fruit and held out the bounty in offering.

I turned my head away, deciding the wall looked more fascinating than his bribe. "What is the matter with you? You've confirmed what I am. I'm here as your hostage. Why push my patience with the threat of mentioning. . . that?"

He ate the chunk of pear when I didn't take it. "You can leave at any time, Eldyn."

I gave him my best unamused gaze.

Arkenu sighed and sliced another thin piece of the pear. "Have I not proven myself to you enough? Only certain people would even know about a dragon's hor—"

"Don't even say the word," I snarled. A horde was a dragon's private business. "And if you knew better, you wouldn't throw such words around."

"I was just wondering how far your loyalty to Thomas was. Perhaps, since you have what you wanted, you've no need of him and therefore are stalling. It would make sense to wait me out. You'll live longer than me."

"I understand your threat perfectly, Arkenu." His leverage over me was Thomas's life. He'd get what he wanted from me easily by stripping me down and stringing me up. But that wasn't what the prophecy foretold. Arkenu needed me to willingly give the knife to him. He needed the symbol of its meaning. He needed me to be his mouthpiece, confirming he was the one prophesized to save all of Neith. But if he really were the one and knew what the prophecy truly entailed, he would not be so eager to claim himself the lost son.

"Let's see what good Thomas is up to, shall we?" Arkenu stood and walked across the room toward me. He pulled out an obsidian sphere from his cloak. Its shiny polish so fine it doubled as a black mirror.

My jaw dropped. My body trembled. My hands jittered as Arkenu dropped a scrying sphere in my palm. A jewel so precious wars had been won by its possessor. "Where did you get this?"

"It was bequeathed to me by my mother." He was going to say more but stopped.

"Do you know what this is?"

He smiled. "Some call it the Eyes of Horus."

Within the eye, a distorted image of my shop appeared. It was like looking through a fishbowl. I turned the eye and saw a bird's eye view of my shop. Thomas was behind the counter speaking with another guild member. William, being a noble, wished to deal with me directly, and his station allowed his eccentrics. There was no sound, but Thomas nodded profusely and twisted his hands over each other. My people needed me, and I couldn't be there.

Arkenu watched the images with keen interest.

"You haven't seen the eye work before?" I asked.

His eyes shifted to me. "A rider's magic comes when he meets his dragon."

I looked up at him through my admonishing eyebrows. Another tit-for-tat game. "If that were true and your dragon were yours, you'd be able to activate Horus's eye."

Arkenu's jaw muscles strained, but otherwise he said nothing.

With a smirk, I handed him the black sphere as if it were no more than an interesting trinket. "He's not yours," I murmured.

"You still persist that I am not the forgotten son, even after I've produced proof, time after time."

"Proof?" I scoffed.

"I'm in possession of Horus's eyes. I've shared secrets only a rider would know. How much more until you relent? I have a mind the think you're holding back the Devil's Dagger out of spite."

"What would you expect?" I threw out a hand. "For me to hand over the chooser of kings? Doesn't that make me the one responsible for at least Aleenia's future? You threatened a man's life. . ."

"I've not hurt him or you."

"I'm starving, Arkenu. That's akin to torture."

"I thought a fast would clear your mind."

"Well, it has! And I'm willing to bet you're not the lost son, nor are you the one that will lead us to safety." My anger got the better of me. But he could not know what the lost son's involvement in the prophecy was, and he'd never guess.

Arkenu held my glare. His cold, black eyes chilled my insides with his calculating measures. Even his temper seemed calculated. We stared at each other until Arkenu held out a whole golden pear. A peace offering.

"Thank you." I took the fruit, for polite reasons, but did not bite into it. I refused.

He leaned against the desk and folded his arms. "If I had not come, what would you have done with the knife?"

"I don't know."

"You wouldn't have sold it?"

"No." Nobody would buy it off me. I didn't want it, but it had to be stashed somewhere safe.

Arkenu sighed. "At least, you have integrity."

I threw up my arms. "Why am I here, Aegis?"

"You don't have to be." He eyed me.

"I'm not giving you the dagger."

"Why not?"

"Because you're not the one." No matter what he said, no matter what "proof" he produced, he wasn't the lost son. The Devil's Dagger should only be left in the hands of someone who didn't want it, but needed to have it. I didn't need it, nor did I want it. That left me as not the right one either.

"But you believe I'm a rider."

A rider? Yes. *The rider?* No. "You're not the forgotten son." I glared at him. In no uncertain terms would I budge on this.

"Then why are you here?" Arkenu cast a hand in the air as if to encompass the city.

"It's personal." Because of the same damnable prophecy, Arkenu tried forcing me to accept his involvement.

"More reason to keep you here. You'll be safe." He sliced off another part of his pear.

I scoffed. If safe meant starving to death, then yeah.

"Tell me about them." Arkenu's tone softened.

"Who?" I cocked my head.

"Ah, a person." Arkenu nodded in knowing fashion. "You're not here for something, but for someone."

Damnable. That was correct. That someone was the dragon I dreamed about every night. Every night the dream was the same.

"It kept bothering me. Why would a drake travel over uncharted seas to come here? There are reasons why people migrate. I thought maybe a refugee. But there are no sanctions for you."

I shrugged. "There's opportunity here." Not a lie. The enclave was desperate for supplies. Another shipment was scheduled to go in two days.

Arkenu watched me looking for my tell like a poker player. "And we can't forget love."

My eyes cast away at the last. Yes, there was that.

The assassin paused. "Interesting."

I glared at him. "Don't pretend to understand my reasons."

"You surprise me, elder." A smile dawned on his face transforming his usually intimidating features. "What's her name?"

I rolled my eyes.

Without missing a beat, Arkenu asked, "Ah, what's *his* name?"

"Go away." I flopped into the newly supplied chair across from the table.

He sat up from the desk and leaned conspiratorially on the wall next to me. "Give me something, Eldyn. I've shared my story."

"If I do, will you leave me be?"

"Just give me a snippet." He held his thumb and forefinger together.

"Promise to go?"

"I'll have the guards bring you dinner."

Resigned, I sighed. "I came to find my dragon."

Arkenu raised his eyebrows. "You're a rider?"

I threw up a hand. "I'm not interested in the dagger. I, unlike some people, do not delude myself that I am the forgotten son."

He gazed at me seeking for more no doubt.

I laid my head back and closed my eyes. That was all I would give. It was too much.

After a moment, Arkenu stood straight and left the room without another word. Dinner was a finely cook steak, mashed potatoes, and a soft roll. But the taste was bitter knowing I'd gained the food with entrusted secrets I wasn't keeping.

CHAPTER 11

ZEROH

STREAMS OF LIGHT CASCADED through thin horizontal windows ushering in the morning. Lullabies played in my mind coiling their notes around my heart. The sweet melody hummed in the background, tucked away in my soul, fading as I awoke to sounds of life.

Birds chirped their praises to the sun. I wasn't used to so much brightness. The dark hole of my room always allowed me to sleep no matter what time of day. But this wasn't my room.

I was chained to a slab of warm, hard stone. A weighty wall of flesh wrapped around my side. The body felt foreign but comforting. Better than being alone.

Blinking the sleep out of my eyes, I focused on Kuval's arm slung over my chest. His leg draped over my thigh. Kuval lay sprawled over me like a blanket. I didn't need warmth, but here he was, wrapped around me like a comma.

"Everything I never wanted," I mused. "Only an idiot would deem it safe to drape himself over a Pyromage. I ought to burn you."

Oh, *fúrr*. Last night. Heat rose up my neck recalling the absolute pleasure I'd had last night. The first like it in a lifetime. And no one had died. At least, to my knowledge, no one had died. Even now my body lay content. After the mind-blowing, body-shattering orgasm, I could stay here on this stone prison with my jailer and retain this cloud-floating euphoria.

Kuval had freed me. Freed the monster inside. Sated my lust. Shown me how to deal with the clawing beast of desire. The ever-present animal in the background tormenting my life. Its hunger normally screeching like the notes of a violin played by a novice. But now the gnawing was silent. Bliss.

His breath shifted from the deep, slow cadence of unconsciousness to the faster rhythm of wakefulness.

"Mmm. . ." He moaned with his eyes closed. "Good morning." He smoothed a hand over my stomach as though he needed to iron wrinkles out of a silk dress.

Then Kuval ruined my quiet moment and slid a hand down my stomach and cupped my balls.

He'd, metaphorically, shoved the screeching instrument back into the hands of the so-called musician. The beast rose, screaming for an encore. The instant hard-on came so fast it peeled the skin off my teeth.

"Wow." Kuval sat up and leaned against his arm. "Your five-year dry spell didn't dampen your libido."

"Shut up." I turned my head and tried getting my lechery under control. After years of abstinence, then having a taste of sin. . . it figured. Gaining control over my erection was not going so well. Now awake, my ornery attitude reminded me of my mission. And so help me I wasn't sure I could go through with it anymore. Kuval wasn't a mission anymore. It was personal.

His languid fingers skimmed my cock and sent my desire skyrocketing.

"Can you not stroke me?" I squinted my eyes and thinned my lips for the most intimidating face I could muster at the not-happening o'clock hour.

He chuckled. "I wouldn't be that cruel to you." He leaned over and suckled on my nipple.

"*Fúrr!*" I bucked and gritted my teeth. I tried to pull my arms down from over my head, but the wrist restraints held me in place.

"So, was last night a usual performance or because you were *backed up*?"

I closed my eyes and relaxed. "I don't know."

"Don't pout. We can find out together." Kuval rose up and straddled me. His usual arrogance replaced by something tender. "You can stop pretending now."

"Pretending about what?"

"Drop the indignant macho act. No matter what you do or say, I know the truth."

"About?" I lifted my eyebrows.

He snorted. "You enjoyed every moment of last night. You screamed my name so many times."

"Did not!" My stomach dropped fearing the truth. I had liked it. I wanted more. But my pride wouldn't let me admit to any of it. I fought the proof because I saw no other way. "You lie."

He laughed. "Do I?" Then he slid two fingers between my ass cheeks and rubbed my puckered hole. "Then why are you pumping out lubricant like a horny teenage girl?"

"What!" I strained against the chains. I would choke him the moment my hands were free.

"Yeah, see. . ." He plunged two fingers inside me. Those two digits slipped inside me as easy as a key into a lock.

To my embarrassment, my cock bobbed in appreciation, and I let out a cry. He didn't stop at just one stroke. He pumped and this time found the bundle of nerves that could short out my train of thought.

I writhed becoming unable to move as the pulsations drilled spikes of pleasure into my brain. The spikes that robbed me of my dignity. In the bright morning sun, Kuval's face dominated my vision.

"Don't hold back, baby. Let go." His husky voice, the perfect aphrodisiac to my long, hard five-year wait for a lover that could handle me. In reality, I never thought I'd find anyone. But now having this, letting Kuval have me. . . I was ruined for life. Abstinence no longer an option.

"Let me take care of you." He grabbed my hip. "Are you ready?"

"Go to hell," I croaked. I would come like a bitch. No stimuli to my cock necessary.

When Kuval uncorked the glass tube and placed it over my cock head, I arched my back, clawed at the stone and screamed till my throat went dry. Saliva leaked from my lips. I could barely focus.

"Feels like you'll get sucked all the way in the tube, doesn't it?" Kuval grabbed another vial.

I shook my head and gasped. "One will do." As soon as I spoke my body convulsed.

My orgasm finished when the vial was filled, but the vial kept sucking. Kuval watched me for a moment, fascinated.

"Off, please." I begged for relief from the vial still trying to pull my cock inside.

He shivered, removed the vial, capped it, and set the large-mouthed tube back in the holding case. Four vials held a red liquid that swirled with angry vindication. Two vials remained empty. My body ached from being told to perform after lack of use. My cock now flaccid.

"Good boy." Kuval gave me a chaste kiss. "Float in your ecstasy. I'll be right back."

I tensed and raised my head. "Where are you going?"

"Don't worry. I'll be sure to take you to the little boy's lavatory." He headed to the opposite side of the room away from the switch of torture.

I puffed out a breath, relieved he walked away from the infernal contraption of bamboo and water. My nemesis.

"Great, now I have to pee. Thanks for mentioning it." But I didn't have to wait too long for Kuval to come back.

When he stepped naked into the small torture chamber, water dripped from his hair, and he smelled like soap. I got a full view of the tattoos rippling over his muscles. They seemed alive as the hypnotic swirls moved along his skin.

"Your turn." He put on a pair of trousers, goggles, and some heavy leather gloves. His pectoral muscles flexed when he grabbed the neck ring lance and placed his feet on either side of my head.

"Can't wait." I glared at him.

He positioned the clamp over my throat. "Lift your head up or this thing will pinch."

I did what he asked, and the metal snapped closed behind the nape of my neck. The chokehold of the shackle helped me forget about Kuval's leering glances.

"Don't bring your junk near my face. I will bite it off."

He smirked, lording over me. "I might like it."

"Deviant."

"Pervert." He stomped on my shackles holding my wrists, and they opened.

"I'm not the one sticking my fingers up a guy's ass."

"But you are the guy enjoying it." He opened my ankle clamps.

I tried pulling my arms down, but my sore limbs tingled from lack of blood flow. Kuval helped lift my torso by pulling me up, neck first, with my fashionable steel necklace. He extended the pole and jammed the pointy end against the stone wall. Guess he didn't want to put holes in the ceiling. That would be bad for me as well. Holes in the bottom of a water tower didn't work out so well for a Pyromage. Hence the reason for me not flaming up and burning Kuval alive while I was sort of free from my bonds.

He massaged my shoulders, working some kind of magic with his strong hands. Those enchanted fingers traveled down my arms until he got to my palms. I felt too mellow to fight. The sex had taken my frustrations down a notch or three. *Fúrr* burned within me, but in a smoldering, passionate way. Not the usual high-tension burn that took a lot of fuel to keep a fire consistent.

Kuval's warm, callous hands wandered downward making all my muscles pliable. He threw off heat like a furnace, and it felt good. While he squeezed the tension from my thighs, I rolled my head, listening to pops and cracks in my spine.

His fingers reluctantly slid away. "Good? Can you walk?"

I opened my eyes and met a soulful, watching gaze. I'd tried to kill this man. He knew I'd try to continue my mission, and yet he didn't reciprocate. I was a prisoner, sure, but was it really that important to him to find out who wanted him dead? "Why are you so kind to me?"

A hand reached up and cupped my cheek. "Am I?"

His touch made me want to close my eyes and nuzzle into the affection. Then his hand was gone. He came around behind me and tied my hands behind my back. The rope itched around my wrists. It was a test. Nothing short of metal could contain my Fúrr.

Kuval came back to my front, took hold of the pole, and pulled it from the wall. At the end of the contraption were little buttons. He twisted the pole till it clicked. The long handle receded inside itself until the lance was four feet in length. I could burn him from being so close if I tried, but I bade my time. Specifically, not a time when I could die as well.

He grabbed a bucket of water and pushed me forward, guiding me from behind. He made me halt at an oak door.

"It's open. Just push."

"How kind of you to let me kick it instead of slamming me through it." Like all the times he bashed my head against walls. To be fair, I *had been* trying to burn him.

The sun hit my naked body in a blaze of glory. Fúrr inside me grew, as if trying to reach its home world.

Pressure on my neck sent me forward into a grass-filled garden. Behind the water tower lay a field of tall oaks, pine, and golden pear trees. There were enough trees to give shade, but spread out enough so we weren't walking through a forest. In the distance, fifty feet away, was a eight-foot-high stone wall.

We walked straight ahead, passing an outhouse and outdoor shower, and deeper into the manicured forest. Beyond the trees lay an odd stone slab nestled up against the wall. A square pocket of concrete floor among paradise.

"That concrete is made with volcanic ash."

"So?"

"So, go ahead and flame up all you want. It won't burn."

Ho, ho, a challenge. I walked up and slapped my feet against the cool surface. Facing this so-called Fireproof barrier, I was made to stand there for several seconds. There didn't seem to be anything unusual about the wall. Like any other, it was made of stone and mortar.

Curious if I was just going to stand here and stare, I craned my neck around to see what Kuval was waiting for.

He was staring at my ass.

A disgusted groan escaped me. I should have known.

"Turn around," he said. A click and scraping sounded through the pole.

I did what he said and turned to face him. The contraption ticked as I moved, and I felt the mechanics of my iron necklace pulse as I slowly twisted.

His eyes raked over me. Within his gray gaze sparked lust and ownership. Possessiveness. With everything he'd done to my body last night I shouldn't be embarrassed, but my face heated. My heart spiked. Excitement. Thrill. Fear. He claimed me.

Me. The one abandoned. The one shunned. The one most undeserving.

It is I that possesses you, my Fire warned. The element didn't speak so much as I felt its desire. *Fúrr* did not want any mistake on who owned who.

"Squat," he said.

"What?"

"Or stand. Doesn't matter. But if you tip the bucket—" He pushed me against the wall. The concrete was not smooth. "Water will spill out."

In defiance, I lowered myself in a chair position. The rough bumps and crevasses on the wall scraped against my skin. Ouch. That took off the old and new.

He pushed a button and the contraption extended out. The pointed end buried itself in a tree behind Kuval. The metal necklace squished me further into the stone. This metal rod defied physics. Metal lances that could extend would get thin at the end, but this pole didn't. Nor did it flex. There was no give.

"Here." Kuval set the bucket of water down below me.

"Are you going to collect my piss and shit too?"

"If your shit comes out burning, that would give new meaning to firebomb."

I couldn't help it. I snickered. "Curious to find out?"

He smiled. "So, you do have a sense of humor. Guess getting laid will do that."

"It's not funny being tied up." My hands, tied behind me, tingled. Finally, my blood flow was coming back.

"You wrote that warrant," he said.

"Yeah, yeah. Your hands got burned. It wasn't that bad." Though I never wanted him to hurt like that again. Seeing his pain was a little too much.

He pursed his lips that was half-smirk, half-rage. "I'm not the princess begging after a few drops of water hit my chest."

"Fuck off."

"Are you offering?"

There was no winning with this guy. "Princess, huh?" I grinned. "You're the one bringing me out here to piss, and for what? To save my dignity?"

"You're a dragon," he said as if that was an answer.

I gritted my teeth. "I'm not a dragon. But there is one thing about Pyromages you have miscalculated."

Kuval wasn't smiling anymore. His eyes fixed me with deadly intensity. "Don't—"

But it was too late. "Pyromages don't actually need to go to the bathroom." I showed him what I meant and let Fúrr envelop me.

I would smell like. . . well, like shit and ammonia, but after a good hot burning, everything wound up smelling like ash. Because everything that wasn't my organs was burned. Including organic waste.

"You might ask yourself," I yelled over the roaring flame. "If Pyromages can't touch water, how do they get clean?"

Kuval stepped back and lowered the pair of goggles over his face.

"Simple," I said. "Fire is the ultimate purification. A Fire that burns hot enough makes everything ash."

Lashes of flame burst out from my body. Uncontrollable. Wild. All consuming.

Irritable licks of plasma scorched the wall that held me prisoner. The leaves high in the trees floated down as cinders. I used every ounce of hate I'd built up and fed it to my

Fire. Kuval took a few steps back, giving me the satisfaction of making the thief flinch.

But all of my loathing wasn't enough. Not enough to burn this damn metal contraption around my neck. My venom was fading, leaving exhaustion in its place. No. Not enough, not enough! I couldn't give in. I searched for the well of grief, agony, rage to feed my Fire. A gambit of shame, regret, nostalgia, all the usual familiars I handed to *Fúrr* as propellant. But I'd used up so much in the initial burst, I was hard pressed to produce the negative, faster-burning emotions.

Pure hate takes a lot of energy to produce, but it burns hot. Hot enough to melt metal. But his contraption still had a hold of me. The only emotions left were those I hadn't felt in a long while. Fondness. Ardor. Love.

Emotion fueled my Fire, but I was hesitant to toss *Fúrr* the softer warmth of affection. As strange as it was, underneath the anger, the shame of being caught by Kuval, the pain he had caused me, there was a warmth for him that radiated from my core. He was kind. Strong. Self-reliant. Positive. Funny. Handsome. Kuval possessed the type of confidence that grew because he lived, breathed, *was* who he wanted to be. Kuval was Kuval. The unstoppable force and the unmovable object.

The source of my tender emotions stood before me, watching with caution. Kuval tortured me, but he hadn't killed me. Not yet anyway. He'd given me pleasure. Touched me when not many dared speak to me. Cared for me. Conversed. Last night's whispered words crowded my head space. He'd asked what I liked, how I felt, all while giving me lascivious caresses, ultimately setting me free.

"Zeroh, I swear I'll bust your head in." Kuval wrestled with the pole device.

My Fire had turned as white as my hair. Holy *fúrr*. White Fire? The hottest I could ever produce before was blue flame, a good two steps cooler than pure white. And this white flame felt easy to maintain. A low hum of energy flowed through me. Neither the rage of hate nor the madness of revenge fueled my Fire. This was pure. Simple. Effortless. Bottomless. So easy, the flames went well over the eight-foot-high wall. Licks of my inferno spread in unison. Fire in harmony. I'd never seen such a sight.

"Zeroh!"

My head was shaken back and forth. The calm sereneness broke.

"Stop!" I shouted.

Kuval gritted his teeth. His forearms bulging. The tattoos on his shoulder rippled. My Fire was hurting him. As the thought crossed my mind, my flames whooshed into nothing. I sagged forward, exhausted. My captor breathed heavily. Kuval gaped open-mouthed at something over my head.

I craned my neck to look at what interested him so much. In the corner of my eye, I saw a huge gaping hole. The concrete around me looked deformed. Heat radiated off the wall. I hadn't been able to melt the damn pole. But I'd *melted* rock. Not just rock, but double-duty, fire-resistant, hardened concrete that might as well be steel.

"Don't. . ." Kuval shook the metal rod.

My knees bent. I started to go down. Sleep would be great right now.

"You sorry son of a bitch." Kuval stained to hold me up by my neck. "I told you not to do that."

Melting a hole in the wall drained me. "I don't have to go pee anymore." I chuckled.

Kuval glared at me through his goggles. He turned on his heel and marched us back inside the water tower.

Delirious and drained, I didn't protest when my feet couldn't keep up with his pace. I tripped, and he dragged me back on my feet none too gentle. We got to the tower, and I was glad for the shade. My feet went for the altar.

"No." Kuval pushed my back against the wall and extended the end of the rod, effectively pinning me to the wall. He took off his thick leather gloves and removed his goggles. Both accessories got thrown on the lab table. He picked up something. I couldn't tell what it was because the metal pole blocked my view. Then I saw him dowse a rag and wring it out.

"Remember, any fire in here, and you'll be dead," he said, anger rolling off his tongue as he stepped next to me.

I had finally managed to piss him off. Go, me.

The rod hissed as Kuval wiped off his contraption. After the metal cooled, he shackled my hands in front, this time with metal, and strung me up on an iron hook bolted to the stone side. It looked like a heavy-duty plant holder that held me a foot away from the wall. I teetered on my toenails to keep the metal bite off my wrists.

Kuval leaned against the door. I must have hurt him. Wanting to view his humiliation, I squirmed and used my toe to turn around.

He heaved with effort. Puffs of smoke accompanied his coughing fit. Soot smudged over him like charcoal sketches. They blended well with his tribal tattoos.

"It's only a matter of time before my guild comes looking for me." Most likely only Arkenu. He would notice my absence. But he was enough. My guild master was the head of the band of murderers, cons, and thieves. It took a considerable amount of respect to wield such a group.

When Kuval turned to me, I knew I was in trouble. His eyes had gone crazy. Not rational. Fevered. His body shook with tremors.

"Let them come," he growled. "I won't be parted from you."

Parted from me? I'd just tried to burn his skin off, and he wouldn't be parted from me? "You are bat-shit crazy." *Fúrr.* I should not have said that. I should have realized he was insane.

He walked over to the box of vials, and with shaking hands, pulled out an empty tube, and closed the box.

"Kuval. . ." My heart pounded.

The thief lifted his wild eyes and roamed my body for what felt like an age. He stalked me with the grace of a noble cat. His feet made no sound. The stillness of the room choked my voice. In increments, he prowled until he could reach out and grab my throat. Kuval's hands roamed my chest down to my waist and over my ass. His touch was cool this time, and oddly comforting.

"Have you ever been taken by a man before?" He pulled me into his chest.

"You know I haven't."

"Then I'm glad I'll be your first."

Oh, *Fúrr.* "Didn't you do enough last night?"

Trembling fingers turned me around. We were chest to chest. His crazed expression turned soft.

Shouting hadn't worked. Insulting him hadn't worked. I tried pleading. "Please. . ." If I said no, I wasn't sure he was in the right frame of mind to not leave me with the Water running.

"Don't be afraid, I won't hurt you." His fingers danced along my ass. His whisper sent a shiver through me. "I won't do anything you don't want."

But if I protested too much, he'd leave and turn on the Water. The choice was mine, and he hadn't hurt me so far.

His fingers circled the globes of my pert, aching bottom. To my disgrace, my hips tilted back, pushing my ass out, asking for his fingers to enter me. Making me feel safe. Wanted. Admired. Despite everything, my cock grew heavy, my breathing turned to panting, and my half-slit eyes cast a drunk gaze. I was too tired to fight.

"All I can do is feed your lust and hope we can get over this screwed up situation." Kuval's face filled with sadness. "You think we can turn this into something more?"

What in *fürr* did he mean by that? What was more?

His hands skimmed over my body sending shivers down to my toes. A finger dipped between my cheeks and rubbed my entrance.

"What are you doing?" I was wet. Dripping. As ready as a wanton teenager. More embarrassing, I groaned. Kuval took it as consent and pushed at my hole.

"Trusting you not to burn my fingers."

"I will. I'll sear them off. You'll pull out brisket." I could if I wanted to. Yet, I couldn't. It was unexplainable.

"You won't." He pressed deeper.

My cock stiffened in response. "I will. . ."

"You already told me your secret, remember?"

"That's right. I kill people." But I squeaked as he pushed his way inside. "Don't think I won't burn off a few appendages. Especially from someone I don't like."

"That's not exactly true, is it?" He pulled back.

Two fingers wiggled firmly inside me, stoking the beast called lust. The other hand caressed my face. His gentle touch made me want to sink into his caress and purr.

"When you walked in that bar I saw you looking at me."

"Because you're my target."

"It was more a look of hunger, a wanting. Not the measurable comparing of another man. I know that look, Zeroh."

"I'm not that interested in you." I arched my back betraying my words.

Kuval slid his finger further inside. "Then why are you slick and ready?"

I kept my mouth shut, squeezing my jaw together, holding the moan bubbling between my solar plexus and my throat.

"Look at yourself." He pulled back just enough to make me miss the heat of his skin. "You're hard. You're wet. You're leaning into my fingers, and you're completely lost in the moment."

"So?"

"Stop hiding behind your shame."

I opened my eyes. "Hiding behind my shame?" The raging torrent of anger rose in my heart. "I don't hide behind it. It's all that I am. I'm nothing without my damn shame."

His sad eyes struck a blow to my heart. I didn't want his pity.

"I kill people." My voice came out a growl. "It's what I'm good at."

"How long have you been an assassin?"

"I've been killing people since I was fifteen."

"Zeroh, how long have you been with the Kenwald guild?"

"None of your business."

"Does being with me make you feel like you're finally being punished?" His usual smile gone. He looked older. Weary. Heartsore.

I flinched. How could he read into me? His all-knowing eyes terrified me. "And that gives you justification for doing this to me?"

"You can say no." His eyebrow lifted in an unspoken chastisement.

I scowled at him.

"You're not refusing me now." He came forward and dipped his finger inside me.

If not for the chains holding me up, I would have fallen into his chest. As I was, my head leaned against his shoulder.

"Damn you." I wanted his lips on me again. "You're wrong. It makes me forget."

Kuval slid behind me. "Vavar was not your fault." He tweaked my nipples sending jolts down my middle, making my cock bob.

"Do what you want," I gritted out. "Just make me forget."

Putting myself in his control gave me a sense of worth. At least, I could give something to someone no matter how insignificant. "Punish me. Ravish me. Shame me. Make me mindless. Do your worst."

His hands shook as they wrapped around my hips. The soft press of lips at the nape of my neck sent a wave of relief down to my core. The knot in my stomach unfurled. My fear was only that. Fear didn't hurt me. I'd been afraid, but Kuval hadn't wounded me. This was so strange. Me, a captive, yet I could kill us both. Which had to be the reason why Kuval's hands shook.

His arms pulled me back into his chest. His hardened nipples scraped along my shoulders. My arms strained against their bonds as my body sank into his warmth. He stuttered a breath that caressed the tangled mess of my hair.

"Are you afraid of me?" My voice so low I sounded more like a squeaking mouse.

"No." He kissed my ear. "This is excitement. What can I say? Your strength gets me off."

"So, knowing I can incinerate your dick the moment you put it in makes you horny?"

He chuckled and kissed my shoulder. "You don't receive much trust, do you?"

Trust. Another thing I wanted but didn't deserve.

"You can trust me," Kuval said. "At least with this."

His words caught me off guard. Yes. That's what I wanted. Trust.

"Trust you? With your cock inside me?" My own words sent a shudder of decadent pleasure through me. I sounded perverse and sexy, and it made my ass clench. How could I be losing my heart and body to this man?

Because save for a few times he'd knocked me into a wall for trying to burn him, he hadn't retaliated against me. Not really. Not while he was with me. Not in the things that counted. The Water torture was for his own safety. He hadn't scorned me for what I was or shunned me. Kuval wasn't wary of my abilities. I was an asset. Not the ticking time bomb everyone tiptoed around or the errant child that could melt off faces.

Kuval took a hand away and probed between my ass. I was going to let him do this. In the back of my mind, I knew I'd enjoy it. His other hand slid down between my thighs and lifted my left leg. I moaned at the pressure against my hole.

I'd never been invaded there like this, but I was wet and willing. More pressure. Then his hard staff breached my port.

"Oh, fúrr."

"You okay?" he said.

I craned my head, breathless and panting. He covered my mouth with his. Our tongues whirling in a dance of mutual enjoyment. Connection. His hips pushed in further. I broke the kiss and cried out. Savoring his taste, I licked my lips and let my head hang forward. "Okay, I'm okay."

"More?"

"Yes."

He buried himself balls deep. The soft pouch of skin tickled my taint. I was right. It felt fantastic. When he pushed in and separated my insides, the invasion stung so good it made my cock tense and jerk against my belly. His started pulling out his massive rod.

"No!" I cried out.

He froze. "Am I hurting you?"

"No! *Fúrr*, no. But I. . . don't pull out. Stay inside me."

His head dropped to my neck. "So, push, don't pull."

"Please."

"You are killing me." He kissed my neck and pulled my right leg into the crook of his elbow.

I was spread wide. Helpless. Tied. Vulnerable. Free.

Kuval pushed inside me. I let some of my own weight settle, using his crotch as my chair. Doing exactly what I'd pleaded him to do, Kuval nudged his way inside me. Stroking me in the deepest part of my body.

"Good boy."

I sighed, letting my head fall. This time I wasn't pissed off at the endearment. White hot sparks burst like fireworks against the darkness behind my eyelids. "I'll come."

"Then come." The response whispered in my ear. He made it sound so easy. Natural. Then a vial slipped over my cock and sucked me into a blissful void.

"Oh, *fúrr*. . . Kuval. . . Kuval. . . Kuval!"

He lifted me up, released my chains from the hook, and started walking. He kept his promise on remaining inside me. No pulling out. In no time, I was on my knees staring at the altar while Kuval pumped inside my ass, his hips moving but never pulling away.

"Zeroh. . ." He bit out. I felt a gush of warmth inside me. He roared out his orgasm.

That was my limit. My cock started filling the vial. I watched in fascination as my cum squirted inside the glass. It was an angry, swirling purple liquid. I swore a tiny fist shook within the mass seemingly to curse my name. I didn't care. As long as it wasn't burning people, it could hate me for all I was worth.

Kuval grabbed the vial and pulled it off me, and I shuddered in relief. The vials never stop sucking even after I'd poured my essence inside.

"Ow, ow, ow. . ." Kuval swore.

I glanced behind me. Kuval swapped the corked vial between hands like a hot potato as he slipped the tube back in the case.

"You okay?" I asked.

"Yeah, it's just hot," he said.

I snapped my head to the vials.

"They're fine." He smiled, but it was a little strained. "See, they're all accounted for. No cracks in the glass. I told you, I've got you." He nuzzled my ear.

Sighing, I let the worry go.

"Now lie down." He tugged at my leg.

He was going to clamp me to the altar again. "I thought you trusted me," I smirked at him over my shoulder.

"Oh, I trust you." He grinned. "To burn things. To try and escape." His smile faded into a softer expression. "To let me make love to you."

Hiding my embarrassment, I turned my head. "Whatever."

The moment I'd had to escape was lost. Not that there had been much of a window. I'd just poured the last of my defiance into a glass vial. There was no way I'd overpower Kuval. Not with this helpless floating contentment. I settled down on my front, allowing him to clamp my ankles and wrists to the altar.

"Why am I face-first in stone?"

"I like looking at your ass."

"Of course."

"It's a nice ass."

"You're an ass," I mumbled.

"Breakfast?"

"Yes."

Why the *fürr* were we having a conversation like lovers when I was chained to an altar? There was something seriously wrong with the both of us.

"So, is my fate forever being a stone warmer, your personal grill, and a cum bucket?"

Kuval came back with a handful of eggs. "Hmmm. . . that sounds awfully domesticated."

I relaxed and let a strange calm wash over my heart. My mind returned to the phenomenon of White Fire, sending flames far and wide without using up the fuel of rage or sorrow. The emotion was a never-ending tap. But that emotion was foreign. Strange. And as of yet, unidentifiable. It wasn't love. It was. . . more. A vast sea of kindling for an eternal flame.

Goo plopped onto my lower back. The sizzle and smell of eggs started wafting into the room. After a moment, there was a scraping along my skin. Kuval flipping the eggs over. Probably with his knife. I was grateful to be spared watching his superior skills with a blade.

"You know, if you said you'd stop trying to kill me, I'd let you go."

"Simple as that? I give my word, and you just drop the chains?"

"Yep." He chuckled. "It's short of physically impossible for a dragon to go back on their word."

"Still on that?" I raised my temperature to cook the eggs on my back. So degrading.

"Still denying it?"

I huffed. Whatever crazy theory he thought, he had me wrong. A dragon? Me? Was it because I could control Fire?

"When's the last time you lied?" he said.

"You don't have to be a supernatural being to own up to a code of conduct."

"Says the assassin." He held out a piece of egg.

I pushed up and took the cooked yolk into my mouth. After swallowing, I said, "What's it to you?"

"How long have you been in Aleenia?"

"Six months." I felt the swish of something along my back and wondered if he had me face down so I wouldn't be nervous about his cooking style.

"Why'd you come here?"

"Oh, you know, once you burn an entire village, it's hard to go back." I'd been on the road searching for a place far away from Burrow Hills. Arkenu had plucked me out of a bar fight, given me a room to stay, a way to make money, and even helped me realize my potential. The guild master had taught me I could control my Fire. Use it. Destroy with it.

"You're not an assassin, Zeroh." His soft insistence pulled at my heart.

"Yes, I am," I whispered. "I am the very essence of death."

"You're no more an assassin than I am."

I pinned him with a glare. "You *are* an assassin."

Kuval laughed and shook his head. "Maybe, one day, I'll introduce you to a real assassin. Me. . . you. . . we still have our souls." He waved another piece of egg in front of my mouth.

"Speak for yourself." I took the offered piece of egg.

"Tell me, have you ever walked out of a bar tossing a firebomb behind your back because the place didn't have your favorite brandy-wine?"

My face screwed up in disgust.

He pointed at me with his knife. "That right there answers my question. No. You haven't. But I knew guys who did."

"Knew?"

"Yeah." Kuval lowered his eyelids and smirked. The implication of past tense was there.

"And you *don't* call yourself an assassin?"

"No. Mercenary is what I am."

"Hired thief describes you best."

Kuval sighed and lifted his knife over my back. I felt pressure and peeling and a leftover stickiness on my skin. Kuval slurped a white-and-yellow mixture of egg into his mouth. We shared the rest in relative silence until the food was gone, and Kuval got up.

Trying to see behind me strained my eye and neck muscles. This whole being naked and strapped down was a little disconcerting.

I tensed when his hand pressed at the small of my back. The hairs on my arms stood up to attention as Kuval started slathering his tongue between my shoulder blades. My heart sped up. Again? Didn't we have sex like twenty minutes ago?

"Kuval?"

"Relax, Sparky."

"Last time you told me to relax, your massive cock split me in half."

"Such a flatterer." He chuckled, then sighed. "I don't think the walls will be able to take it if I let you fire up."

"I'd rather have food stuck to me."

"Fine." He got up and tinkered around behind me.

When he came back, a damp cloth wiped my back. I waited for the burn. Nothing. The wetness from the towel didn't cause pain. I turned my head and eyed Kuval behind me.

"Pure lemon juice. Does it hurt?"

When had he squeezed lemons? "No."

"Good." He left and tinkered around until he brought over my ancient book and lay on top of me. He held most his weight on his elbows but the lower half of his body pressed me deeper into the stone.

"What are you doing?"

"Read to me." He parted my legs and nestled himself so I could feel his bare chest on my back, his soft but large cock under his trousers, and his warm toes skimming my calves.

"Stop wiggling," he said. "You're as squeamish as a virgin princess. I'm bored. That's all. Entertain me."

I covered my contented sigh with a huff. His proximity sent a rush through my veins. His weight, his skin, and his steady rhythmic breathing soothed the anxiety radiating from my core. The more he calmed my nerves, the more my reaction worried me. A contradiction, yet the cycle was beginning again. I felt guilty at yearning for him.

He propped the book up against the wall and opened it to the page I'd been reading when we met at the bar.

Kuval stilled.

"What's wrong?"

"Nothing. Read."

I started at the top of the page. "The Devil's Dagger—"

"That's what it's called?"

"Do you want me to read?"

He blew in my ear, sending shivers down my spine. "Fine. Go on."

"The Devil's Dagger is not a knife of the living. Its sole purpose is to fill demons into the flesh of humans."

Kuval swore.

I ignored him. "Once inserted into a person, the demon can take control. The holder of the knife is said be able to wield a demon army."

As I looked at the words I had this strange feeling. "This is wrong."

"What?" Kuval leaned over and looked at my profile.

"Yeah, this is wrong. The words are there but it's like. . ." I paused trying to sort out my inner turmoil.

"Like a lie?" Kuval supplied.

"Yeah." I glanced over at him.

He squinted at the page. "What's that word?" Kuval pointed at the top left of the page.

"The."

"And that one?" He moved his pointed finger right.

"Devil's."

"That one?" He again skimmed to the next word.

"Dagger."

"Hmmm. . ." I stared as if he were trying to burn the words into memory.

"Do you want to learn to read?"

"Well. . . since you're offering. . ." He grinned.

I laughed. Maybe I'd struck a chord jabbing at his illiteracy. He'd been so nonchalant I thought he might be too proud to learn. But here he was, confusing me again with his eager enthusiasm.

"A bit hard to teach with no limbs to use."

"You'll manage."

"Fine. Turn the page."

He did.

"Top left corner, that's 'a.'"

As I explained the alphabet, and what each squiggle meant, the character's origin and the particular sounds of each letter, we swiftly went into combinations. After connectives, I taught him vowels, consonants, verbs, nouns and sentence construction. By the time the sun kissed the horizon its final goodnight, I was convinced. Kuval was a certified genius. He had learned the alphabet, and could read easy sentences within a day. Each time my quick studier surprised me, and I confessed my amazement, Kuval blushed and his eagerness resumed.

During the lesson he'd put me back on the heavy-duty candelabra hook thing so we could both stand and look at the page together. His warm skin at my back and our accidental touches weren't sexual, until he closed the book and sagged into my small frame.

"We need brain food." Kuval slid his hand around me and placed his palm on my stomach. "You've been dutifully teaching me. I bet you're exhausted."

"You're the one who should be exhausted. Learning isn't easy. Your brain has to be mush." I was still naked, but the low burn inside me kept us both warm in the clammy room.

"Unless you need some relief." He nipped the underside of my upstretched arm.

"What a lecherous old man you are." *Fúrr*, I must be brain dead, flirting like this.

"Mmmm. . . food first. Then I can do my best to make you faint again."

"That's not fair. . ." I sputtered. "I was exhausted."

His chest rumbled in mirth. After he checked his larger-than-life sack, he pulled out potatoes, chicken breast, and carrots. I narrowed my eyes.

"That looks suspiciously like stew."

Kuval smirked and laid the contents on the lab table. When I was strapped back to the altar, he brought out a pot. Ung. I knew it.

"I swear. . . if I get splattered with water. . ."

"Calm, Sparky. I won't fill the water all the way."

By the end of the night, my stomach was full, my body satiated, the last vial filled, and my personal blanket wrapped around me as I drifted to slumber.

CHAPTER 12

ELDYN

THE FLOATING HUMAN FORM of my dragon twirled in lazy spirals far beneath Water's surface. He remained still, lifeless, deep within his element. Even though we were under water, a voice deep with longing sang a tune I hummed whenever my hope started to fade.

For the past fifty years, I'd had this same dream. I'd memorized it, him, and everything in context. But no matter where I searched during my travels, no matter the town, village, or cities, dreams were the only place I saw him.

He was my goal, my life's work, my intended, and the reason I ventured into unknown territory away from home, away from my kind, and away from the responsibilities as elder to my people.

Books floated between us. His short white hair drifted around his gaunt face. The tails of his black coat wandered behind him. His white shirt open, revealed his alabaster skin from neck to navel. He was painfully thin. I guessed him young, not yet over his adolescent years. His black pants were unbuttoned at the top, the current playing with the open flaps, teasing me, drawing my attention. Watching always made me curious if his pants would float off altogether. Untied shoelaces drifted in the water as if a typhoon interrupted us during a session of playful intimacy.

I could touch him, sing to him, sway with him in the water, but he never responded. Another infuriating fact was that he never opened his eyes. I'd recognize his face in the waking world, but his eyes. . . I wanted to see the waterfall in his eyes.

My duty was to find him and bring him back. To be with us. To rule. To lead Neith to its final place. I would guide him, and he would deliver the world to its intended destination.

Duty, a promise, and my conscious kept me from wandering in freedom or going back to Ekinphrow. Homesick for drake companionship, yet I could not go back to stay there without *him*. Especially not with these dreams of him.

Taught in prophecy, I interpreted the dream metaphorically. Water was his element, that was clear. The books meant learning or knowledge, maybe? I took it as a sign he wanted me to learn the ways of elemental Water. I had, still did, abandoning Air for his elemental discipline. His state of undress confirmed he was not ready for me yet. Still. Even after all this time.

If he'd just open his eyes, see me, look at me, then maybe he could find me. Or I could find him. We could be together and figure out the rest. But the dream came more and more with a sense of urgency.

In my dream, I swam over and cupped his face. *Wake up. I'm right here. Tell me what you need me to do. You're my dragon. I know you're mine. Do you not feel our bond?*

He reached out, groping.

Damnable! A change in the dream. He'd never done this before. I caught his hands, and he embraced me with an expression of desperation—still his eyes were closed. *I'm here. I'm here.* Desperate, clinging, searching. *Please. Tell me where to find you.*

We floated for a while holding each other. His arms pinned me to him making me feel like the one needing security. Maybe I did. Could he feel through the bond how much I needed him right now? How my faith in searching for him waned after so long. Was this reassurance? A sign?

No matter. Now I knew what it felt like to be held by my dragon. He was warm. Most of that warmth came from within me. But the Water around us was not the bone-seeping cold of the deep. Heat radiated off him. Thank the elements, perhaps I wouldn't be subjected to a future of freezing temperatures.

Why I never sought him in the ocean I couldn't pinpoint. I just *knew* he was above Water level. Knew it like I knew the seasons would change.

Laying my head on his chest, I gripped him tighter. *Do you know I'm weary of my travels? Can you tell me when we will meet? Where I can find you?*

A vicious tide forced us apart. The Water swelled pushing him down into darkness.

I panicked. I clawed. I fought to reach him.

Gone. He was gone. *No!* I would not let him disappear so easily. Even in my dream, Vesi assisted me. Water swirled around me like a hurricane, propelling me down. I chased after my dragon through the void. My element pushed me, helped me follow where he'd gone, but I could not see him. My dragon was nowhere.

Debris floated around me. Books languished in Water. Parts of a chair, an armrest here, the back side there, slowly rose to the surface. A desk rested on the ocean floor. But it wasn't the ocean—it was a stone room with no door. No windows. Like me, books hung in the room like drifting water-logged butterflies. The room seemed familiar. One of the books rocked side to side, its pages shifting with the tide. I reached for it. . .

I woke with a start. This was not my bed. It wasn't even a bed, it was a chair. My back muscles groaned from being bent over a table. My arm tingled in protest for being used as a bookmark. My hand covered an illustration of the Devil's Dagger.

My dragon. Something was horribly wrong. Beads of sweat ran down the nape of my neck. Yes, something was wrong. Wrong with my dragon.

I leaped to my feet and ran to the door.

"Arkenu!" My fists pounded on the wood. "Arkenu!"

Damnable. I grabbed the latch and opened the door, but I didn't place a toe out of the room. "Master Aegis!"

The guard outside jumped to his feet. It was the same shadow as before.

"Get your guild master, now," I snarled.

"Ever-loving hell, a bit late for a talk, mage," the shadow spat.

"Retrieve Master Aegis." I pulled on Vesi, ready to make good on a threat that teetered into my mind.

"It's the middle of the night. I'm not disturbing him now."

"Go get him." I didn't care if it was All Saints' Day. I needed to get to my dragon.

"No."

"Damnable. . . I will make you." I'd seen a Hydragon control a person before. Didn't mean I could, but it wouldn't stop me from trying. Not when my dragon needed me.

"Can I hope you've figured everything out and are desperate to claim me my right?" Arkenu strutted from the shadows.

"Arkenu." I clasped my hands together. "Please, I need to go."

Steel eyes assessed me. "Hand me the dagger, and you are free from your obligation."

No. I couldn't stay here, and I couldn't give him the relic.

My bond, my promise held me in the room. Sure, I could physically walk out, but if I did, no element—not Water, not Air, not any of them would ever serve me again. With or without my dragon, after breaking a promise, the elements would consider me persona non grata. All my searching, all this time, changing my course in elemental studies, everything was slipping away.

I dropped to my knees and held my hands together, begging, praying Arkenu would understand. "Please, Arkenu, Master Aegis, I need to go. . ."

"Dagger first." Staring back with haughty, cold eyes Arkenu held out his hand.

I shook my head. "Please," I whispered, bowing. "My dragon. . . my dragon needs me."

Arkenu squatted, his expression drifted to pity, hurt, and sorrow before he closed his eyes. "Dagger."

"Damnable, I swear I will return, but I must find him."

"Leave if you must, but I cannot guarantee Thomas's safety."

I hit the stone floor with a fist. "You know I can't leave this room. Not without your exoneration."

"Your magic is a small price to pay, if what you say is true and your dragon needs you. Go to him."

"Aegis." I was getting angry. He taunted me, left me with no choices. "Aegis. Aegis. Aegis," I chanted. Aegis—protector, shelter, refuge for the people. I called on the Aegis and his duty, bound by title. My mantra sparked anger in him.

"Enough! All dragons are safe here. I have always provided safe haven. There is no need to invoke my responsibility. If I knew who your dragon was, I'd bring him here to safety."

"I must find him." My panic was a cloying taste settling at the back of my throat.

"Then choose your sacrifice."

Rage burned. "Damn you." I pulled on Vesi, attacking Arkenu through his own blood, mixing it with air. A painful way to die.

Arkenu rushed forward. My back was on the floor. My jaw ached. The world spun.

"Just think how bonded you'll be to your element for remaining true to your word after such a dilemma." Arkenu's face filled my vision. He patted at my chest, my sides, and my sleeves, looting me as if I were dead.

"Looking for something?" My own words swam inside my ears. It was then I really felt the pain of his strike to my chin that knocked me down. Stone, cold and hard pressed against my back.

"I know you have it." He patted my chest and arms, not giving up his search. He was undoubtedly trying to snake the knife from me.

My smile reached to the point of painful. "You'll never find it."

"Protecting myself does not devoid you of your promise to stay," he huffed and shoved my sleeves up. "This robe is enchanted."

As my head cleared, I swatted at his intruding hands. "You hit me." I laughed, getting over the stun of being punched.

"You won't hand it over, not even for your dragon?" He lifted a brow.

"Especially not for him." An idea formed in my head. "And I won't hand it over to you."

Arkenu sighed. "Very well." He stood and walked to the door. "Stay here and rot."

"Wait!" I reached out, grasping to stop him. "Your Pyragon, Zeroh." Why didn't I think of this before?

Arkenu turned. "Yes?"

"I will give him the dagger, if he is indeed a dragon."

He narrowed his eyes and stepped closer. "You will give it to him?"

"Yes. If he sees fit to give it to you, then you'll have it." I held my breath. It was the only compromise I could think of and not much of a risk for me. A dragon would never hand the dagger over to anyone but the forgotten son.

The Aegis stared at me hard for half a minute. "You believe the dagger will be safe with him."

"It will be." Because a dragon would never want the responsibility of the dagger.

"You're so sure he won't just hand it to me?"

"Every dragon knows the significance of the dagger," I huffed. "He won't give it to you unless you're the heir."

Only a dragon could be trusted with the Devil's Dagger. Even I was tempted to use it for my own gain. If it was handed to Zeroh, and he was a Pyragon, then my duty to protect it, to keep it out of human hands would be fulfilled. I could get out of here and help my Hydragon.

Arkenu eyes danced in calculation. "Then I will bring him here."

I couldn't deny the smirk on my face. "I thought '*you asked, he grants.*'"

He rose without responding.

"If I give him the Devil's Dagger, you will let me go?"

"Yes."

"And Thomas?"

"Will be left alone."

"Agreed then."

Arkenu marched out of the room, closing the door. This time he latched the deadbolt.

CHAPTER 13

ZEROH

"Please don't go. I'll do anything. Anything!" I pulled at my chains, frantic, panting, eyes darting from Kuval's face to the bamboo contraption.

He was doing his best to be carefree about the situation, but he refused to look at me. "We're out of food," he said. "And vials."

"Take me with you. I'll be good. Your good boy. I swear. I promise. Just don't turn that spigot."

He winced, but nothing I said made Kuval listen to me.

"You said. . . you said dragons don't lie. I. . . I'll promise. Please." My voice rose to a pitch that would make a sparrow's ears hurt. "Please!"

It wasn't working. He'd shut me out. Kuval was going to turn and leave, and when he did, the water would flow. I had to do something. Say something. Anything to break through to his indifference. I mustered a firm, steady voice as he opened the front door.

"I will suck your cock. I will guzzle your cum. Not a drop will spill from my mouth. You can bend me to my knees and shove that massive snake in your pants down my throat for as long as you like without a single complaint from me."

He paused and stood in the doorway without looking back. Three seconds passed. His hand clutched the knob.

"No biting. No tricks. No Fire," I continued. "You'll beg for more, and I will open my mouth to you like a *fúrr* damn baby bird. Gladly. But only if you *take me with you now*."

Kuval swore, turned, and shoved the door closed. Stomping over to me, he loomed over my body. "Swear to me you will not flame up, heat yourself, burn anyone or anything, or hurt me while we are out."

"For this outing, I swear I will not so much as heat my skin. But aside from you, I reserve the right to protect myself."

"No." He swept his hand as if batting the idea away.

"Kuval, I'm an assassin. . ."

"You must trust me. I will protect you. No flames. No heat. No balls of fire. Not without my permission. No matter what."

I clenched my teeth. *Fúrr*, he was leaving me defenseless. "There are people out there that would kill me."

"Then you'll be safer here." He turned.

"No! Okay. No flames." What the hell was I doing? Staying the *fúrr* away from Water, that's what. "No heat. No fireballs. No matter what. Nothing. Not without your express permission."

"And I get to pick when and where you give me the pleasure of... shoving my snake down your throat." The smile on his face shone just as brightly as his laughing eyes.

I swallowed. "Fantastic. Public humiliation, huh?"

His expression softened and a finger caressed my lips. "No. I like doing it outside, but not with strange eyes on me and my lover."

Lover. My eyes widened. Another swallow. I cast my gaze elsewhere. "Fine."

Kuval double-timed it, and I was dressed in my black pants, black coat, black boots, and white shirt. Of course, a certain silver necklace-manacle completed the ensemble. Wonderful. This was its own public humiliation. I could hear the hoots and hollers of the towners now. *Got yourself a Fire eater? How much for allowing me to dowse 'em?*

No. Kuval wouldn't do that to me, would he? Had I traded one Water torture for another?

Faith. He wanted faith. A part of my heart wanted so desperately to trust. While the broken, hardened part of me cursed my stupidity. Hope was a fragile aphrodisiac. The kind where, in the past, I'd expected euphoria and received misery. It might not have been so bad if he'd left my hands free, but shackles clamped around my wrists.

"I don't want shop owners claiming you a thief."

"I'm not going to steal anything."

He gave me a pointed stare.

"As you wish." I shrugged. It was to be expected. At least, my feet were free.

"I do wish." He gave me an inviting sideways grin, and we set off in the bright early morning.

I'd never really seen Aleenia much during the day. Arkenu had sequestered me on the Brogan grounds for my safety. He had said people wouldn't take my presence well, and I had believed him. My first encounter with an Aleenian resident started with a fist fight. Arkenu ended our tiff with a crooked eyebrow and a few words.

Aleenia's beautifully curved, wide streets were filled with appreciative merchants selling wares from tents in every available space. But she was an old city, and no one had tended to her health. Aleenia's crumbling walls, shattered cobblestone streets, and run-down state was more obvious in sunlight. During the nights, I'd prowled in darkness, thankful for the broken windows in abandoned apartments, crates, and debris in the alleyways, and the uneven skyline of crumbling buildings. They'd shielded my form and hidden my movements.

But seeing her in daylight was much like waking up to a whore after a night of debauchery. The nighttime activities might be fun, but the wrinkles, sunspots, and blemishes were hard to ignore on her face in the harsh light. Yet, I still loved her. Like people, Aleenia had other facets to her. She wasn't just a city, she was also an adored mother. Her buildings were home to many people. The merchants claiming their space on her streets were proud. None condemned the city for its disrepair. They just weren't wealthy enough to bring her back to shape.

"This city was built around a dragon, so don't be too harsh on her." Kuval craned his neck and eyed me. He spoke often of the dragon the city had been named for and who had protected a group of villagers centuries ago. Or so he said.

"I wasn't thinking ill of her." If a dragon's size wasn't exaggerated as being large as mountains, then Aleenia herself would not have been able to roam even these wide streets. The roads were wide enough for a carriage, but the cobblestone road ruined more wheels than it was worth.

Kuval avoided those cul-de-sac alleys and opted to choke me with his maniacal contraption along the busy main roads. I tiptoed the best I could but did not find much purchase under my feet. My captor had slung the rod over his shoulder and didn't look back. If I were three feet taller, I might be able to walk comfortably. I doubted that was what Kuval wanted. Still. . .

"Ku. . ." I choked out. "Ku. . . vah. . ."

He turned one eye to me. "Promise you won't try and escape?"

"Didn't. . . I. . . already?"

Kuval turned forward and stepped up his pace.

"Yes. This. . . outing. . . yes."

"Yes what?" He lowered the bar.

I could breathe. After a few gulps of air, I said, "I promise I won't try to escape. Now, can I please walk on my own without you dragging me by my neck?"

"It's a compliment, ya know."

"What? Being choked?"

His shoulders jiggled as if he were laughing. "Showing you my back means I trust you. Demanding a promise means I think highly of your intelligence and power."

Okay. I understood him showing his back to me but. . . "How is a promise showing me you think I'm clever?"

"Really?" He shook his head. "If it weren't for your eyes, I'd be fooled into thinking you *were* human."

"Thanks?" I flinched. The mention of what made me stand out wasn't a compliment. Not to me.

"You're smart. Figure it out." He lowered the pole, holding it so his arm was at his side. The angle at least allowed me to breath and walk.

"Even so, help me out."

"Do you know why you don't lie? Why you keep your promises?"

"Because my word is all I have left."

"That ethic is ingrained in you." He shook his head. For a moment, I thought he flashed me a look of awe. "Magic is so much your essence you just can't, can you?"

I shrugged.

"How did you get so powerful without knowing the rules?" His brows crinkled.

"What rules?" I tried to jam a part of my coat between my skin and the contraption so the metal wouldn't rub against my neck. No luck.

"The rules of magic. The elements. Your Fire."

I narrowed my eyes, repeating, "What rules?"

He huffed. "Your word is your bond, right?"

"Yes." Everyone knew that.

"What happens when you lie? When you break a promise?"

I shrugged. "Your words can no longer be trusted."

"How?" he asked me, like it wasn't obvious.

"People find out, eventually. Then they don't take you at your word anymore."

"Good." He nodded. "Imagine the elements are people. Well, four people, and word gets around faster than a mouse can eat cheese."

"Sure."

"Those four people aren't going to trust you, right?"

"I see what you're saying." Made sense. I never had the urge to say or do something other than what I wanted. "How do you know so much about *the rules*?"

Kuval pinched his eyebrows together and shrugged. "I just do. I always have."

He turned his back to me, and we entered the main road. Kuval shortened the distance between us. A crowd of people flowed in the street. The smell of unwashed beggars blasted my nose. I kept my head down, closed my fire-burning eyes, and allowed Kuval to guide me.

Through the slits of my eyelids, I watched merchants shouting about their wares from their respective cloth pavilions. Some had fruit. Others meat. Baguettes waved in the air. Cloths, flags, and tents formed a sea of color.

Nobles mixed with merchants. Merchants spoke with peasants. Peasants begged. The wealthy bought food and wares. The middle-class sold goods. But all the classes spoke with one another. There was tension between the wealthy and the poor but generally, people seemed to accept the vast differences of their lifestyles.

The streets were filled with bodies. People danced around each other, dodging shoulders twisted, torsos slinked past, but people gave Kuval and I a wide berth.

"Jacob, don't!" a woman yelled.

A child the height of my thigh darted under the metal bar between us, and the woman screeched at the boy. She hurried around us, over to him, and swatted his behind for his defiance. She never looked back at us, but the boy grinned in triumph.

A man in a black frock, black vest, and purple paisley ascot approached Kuval. He was a noble if I ever saw one. He pranced with the air of opportunity and looked at both men and women with speculative interest, like he was searching for his next meal.

"Good morning, Kal," the man said to Kuval in a high-pitched, light tone.

Kuval kept walking. I didn't have the opportunity to see the thief's face and couldn't tell if he was pleased or dismayed to see the man.

The Dandy kept pace with him and chatted about nothing. They were evenly matched in height, and each was the polar opposite of the other. One tattooed half-naked barbarian, and the other finely dressed, well-bred noble.

"How much for the laborer?" The noble eyed me up and down.

The ugly temptation to snarl at him that I was no slave nearly made me forget the promise not to ash anyone.

Kuval cocked a grin at the man. "He's not for sale."

I preened. That's right. I was his. Oh, *fŭrr*. Why should I be happy about that? But Kuval's refusal got me a knowing, lascivious look from the Dandy. I didn't appreciate his perusal.

"Oh," the man breathed. "Too bad."

Kuval laughed. "Take a closer look, William. You wouldn't be able to handle this one."

Of course. Kuval was showing me off. . . *look what I caught. A big bad Pyromage.*

The Dandy glanced at me, and I lifted my eyes to him and stared back.

The noble flashed a grin. "My, my. The king will be so pleased you've captured a dr—"

"What news do you have about the shopkeeper?"

William sniffed. "The Hydromage?"

"Yes, Will," Kuval said, without patience. "Where is Eldyn?"

"Haven't seen him for days. He won't take my calls." The Dandy's indignant response told me he was upset someone would deign not to receive him.

"Thomas hasn't said where he is?"

William shook his head. "Not a word."

"Great," Kuval snorted. "What good are you?"

William squeaked. "I'm still looking. I can only push so *hard*." The Dandy grinned at the last word.

My mind raced. Kuval was looking for a Hydromage named Eldyn. Why? Did it have to do with me? It was also the second time I'd heard the name Eldyn. It resonated within my soul.

"Look a little harder, yeah?" Kuval did not look happy.

"You're no fun today." William sighed.

"Don't say anything about him." Kuval tossed a thumb at me.

"Wouldn't think of ruining your surprise. But don't you think parading him around might get him noticed?" William didn't wait for an answer and broke off from us leaving me with questions. None of which were appropriate to ask right now.

"What do you want with a Hydromage?" I asked.

Kuval kept walking, remaining silent.

"Who's Eldyn?"

He turned his head and gave me an eye roll. "They really have been keeping you in a hole."

I tsked and mumbled, "I burn people, remember. Not much social interaction there."

We stopped at a small market where a tented display housed fruit. Most shops supported second- and third-story apartments. Cracks in the concrete would make me nervous living inside these ancient homes. But several people cast gazes out from their bay windows.

As I stood while Kuval shifted through fruit, a blond, brown-eyed man came out wiping his hands on a dirty apron. "Hey, get that thing out of here."

Kuval looked up. "What?"

"I said. . ." The shopkeeper pointed to me. "Get that thing out of here."

Crap. I should have kept my eyes closed. I sighed and shifted my gaze downward. "Come on, Kuval. I know a place that won't mind my presence."

"No." Kuval turned to the shopkeeper. "So, let me get this clear. You are telling me that my coin is no good here because you can't treat him like a respectable sentient be-ing?"

The shopkeeper eyed me with suspicion. "Your coin is fine, but we don't serve his kind here."

The back of Kuval's neck grew red. "Are you trying to piss him off? You know he could wipe your store away in a fire-ridden tornado, and you still won't let him in?"

"Kuval, let's go." I tugged at the pole. Nobody's mind was changed by force. It took reason. Something a terrified man did not possess.

"That's why he's not allowed in my shop." The man's chin rose in defiance.

"He's not an—"

"Animal?" The shopkeeper finished Kuval's sentence. "Son, I know exactly what he is."

"Oh, so you know what he is, do you? Do you know what Aleenia means?"

Why was Kuval being so obstinate? I tugged on the manacle.

"What?" The shopkeeper went from bold to angry.

"Go on, tell me. Tell me what Aleenia means. You don't know, do you? It means origin. Do you remember Yair's mother? The one everyone in this city owes a debt of grat-itude to? The one this city was named after?"

"Son, I don't need a lesson in history. I want you and *that* out."

Kuval gripped the metal pole. It was then I noticed the thief had the point to the extendable end towards the shopkeeper's chest. This wasn't right. The shopkeeper had a say in who he partook in business.

"Kuval," I said with as much dignity as I could muster. "We could be doing something *else*."

Finally, he looked back and hit me with a look of protectiveness. "Fine."

I tried to give the shopkeeper a look of understanding. He wasn't the first nor the last that wouldn't want an unstable firebomb in his establishment. Barkeep was an exception. Not the rule.

Kuval's shoulders tensed, and I could barely make out his mumbling.

"It doesn't matter," I said.

He stopped and turned. "It matters to me."

"Why?"

"Because. . ." The sharp angry shine in his eyes softened. "Because once you would have been revered, not shunned."

"I've done nothing to make anyone revere me. In fact, just the opposite."

"It's just wrong."

"Why?"

Kuval gave me a huff and walked.

The next cloth pavilion he chose to enter, the shopkeeper was either too afraid to ask me to leave or didn't care. Kuval bought steaks, eggs, and fruit enough for two to eat over four days. Anything more would spoil. At least, he planned on keeping me alive for that long.

As we walked the streets, we traveled further into the less-worn paths. Fewer people roamed here, but I still kept my gaze down. The shops were permanent structures as opposed to tents.

He opened one of the rickety front doors, and we entered the shop with a well-loved interior.

Books shelves lined up in rows. Kuval turned right around a bookcase and then left between a wall and shelves leading me against the very last row. He pushed me against the wall and deployed the pole extension. The span between was twenty feet. To my right was a display cabinet. An actual glass display cabinet. A luxury one didn't see every day. Kuval stepped up to the counter comfortable as if he belonged behind the cabinet showing off the wares. He greeted the man standing in wait.

"Hey, Thomas. Is Eldyn in?"

Thomas was an older gentleman with pepper hair, bulging muscles, but a soft way about him. "No, sir, just me."

Kuval smiled and pulled out a vial. The red iridescent liquid stirred inside the tube. Oh, *furr*. He had that all this time?

"Holy hell, where did you find Fire essence?" The older gentleman put on a leather glove and inspected the vial. "Hooo. . . wee. . . that's one angry element in there. How much?"

Kuval leaned over the glass case and set his elbows on the surface. "Free if you tell me where Eldyn went."

Thomas's excitement deflated, and he tried handing the vial back to Kuval. "I haven't seen the master for days."

Kuval waved the *Fire essence* away. "Thomas, I know you know where he is."

The older gentleman shook his head. "Even if I did, I know he doesn't want to see you."

Kuval stood up and raked a hand through his hair. "I wish I knew why."

Thomas raised his bushy eyebrows. "You don't know?"

"Of course not. If I did, I'd be pleading my case. Thomas, what did I do?"

"All I know is you came in with that box, and before I knew it, he was gone."

"But he told you where he was going?"

Thomas shook his head again. "He's gone. That's all I know."

Kuval's head hung low. "I need to talk to him."

Thomas shrugged. "Can't help you."

"I need more vials."

"Now *that* I can help you with." Thomas's smile returned. "How much for the Fire essence?"

"Nine gold."

I coughed. Nine gold? For my. . . ummm. . . did Thomas know what Fire essence was?

Kuval smirked over at me. I could just see the calculations going on in his head.

"Five gold," Thomas said.

"Eight with the promise of another filled vial in a few days and as many corked Ether as you got."

"Same quality?" Thomas inspected the vial like a jeweler would a diamond.

Quality? I wanted to crawl in a hole.

"Absolutely." Kuval grinned.

Thomas handed over the vials and eight gold—eagerly. He might not be so quick if he knew what that vial really held.

I was freed from the wall, and we started down the row as Thomas called after Kuval, "Is it true what they say about Fire essence?"

Kuval laughed without looking back. "Every bit."

***

Kuval turned us down a cul-de-sac alleyway only good to those who lived in the crumbling complexes. Trash collected at the base of the buildings. Glass, cloth scraps, and pieces of wood littered the street.

Nervous as to the deed to come, I asked, "Does Thomas know what he just bought, *for eight gold*?" Holy *fúrr*, that was an exorbitant amount for. . . cum.

"Like I said. . ." Kuval grinned back at me. "People always think dragon essence is blood or tears. They think it's something inside that has to be extracted. As if I have to kill you to get it."

Little did they know. "What do people do with it?"

He laughed. "They never go cold, that's for sure."

Sigh. "What are you going to do with the other five?" He could sell them. For one gold, he could buy ten whores for a night of mayhem. Yet here he was dragging me down a dirty alley to get me to suck him off. I wasn't going to pretend he'd forgotten about our condition. Nor would I lie to myself this was not that moment of truth.

We got to the dead end, and Kuval turned around. He swung me so my back was against stone. Behind him was the opposing building. To my right was the alley's third wall. The cul-de-sac was empty. No life inside the apartments above. No eyes peeked from windows. No children shouting in play. No one here to save me from my fate.

I was terrified. But Kuval didn't frighten me. It wasn't just the fact that he made my palms clammy and my breath hitch. No. It was how much my mouth watered, how the hair on my arms rose like needles stuck in my skin, how my heart sped up and raced alongside the images in my head. I was not afraid of Kuval or what he would do. I was out-of-my-mind petrified of my reaction to him.

Kuval's half-lidded gaze cast longingly at my mouth. When he licked his lips, my cock twitched.

Fúrr. I do not want this. I do not want this. I do not want this.

Each unconvincing mantra did nothing to stint my growing arousal. If I gave in to this, I might as well be branded as his. He'd had me in nearly every way, but this. . . this was different.

Intimate.

The last barrier to admitting I liked what he gave. *Fúrr.* My future was being tied up in Kuval's basement getting off with him inside me. The thought *wasn't* unpleasant. Lost in a world of pleasure. Nothing to worry for except the next time he'd leave and turn on that water pipe. Therein lay the problem.

All it would take was one slip and an entire town would burn. If I got comfortable with feeling this kind of desire, I'd become more dangerous than ever. It was bad holding myself back and yearning for release. But now, knowing his touch. Recalling the memory of his fingers gliding down my sides soft as a lover's touch. I had to escape sooner rather than later.

Kuval lifted his fingers and pinched my chin. His wayward thumb ran along my lips. "Open."

I parted my mouth, and his thumb pressed lightly down on my tongue.

"Suck."

Careful not to bite, as promised, I wrapped my lips around his digit.

"Harder."

I sucked until my cheeks hollowed.

"Good. Just like that. Now, close your jaw a little."

"Mmmm?" I appraised him.

"Featherlight, let me feel the barest skim of teeth."

Oh. A rush of embarrassment heated my face. He was showing me how he liked it. I fought not to swallow—and failed. That gave too much away. But I did what he asked. Enjoying the torment, all under the guise of my promise.

"Good boy," Kuval whispered. His eyes heavy with lust. The endearment grew on me. Still. . .

"I'm not a pet."

"Kneel." Kuval's gaze morphed into a dangerous lechery. As if he'd do me harm if I moved the wrong way.

My jaw went slack. This was the side to Kuval I found irresistible. Thinking better of back-talking, I shut my mouth and lowered to my knees. My breath heavy pants. My cock hard and testing the band of my trousers. Compliancy as my scapegoat, I was freed of judgment.

He set a hand at the back of my head then twisted the bar of my neck manacle. The stick extended and punched a hole into the wall behind him. From neck to head, I was confined to brick and mortar. His hand saved my brain from getting slammed back. His warm grip preferable to being knocked into the wall.

Looking up at him from this angle allowed me to see the full effect of my acquiescence. His pupils were blown. His eyes fevered, a glaze of need filmed over the usually silver irises. His chest heaved. His cock, hard and dead center of my vision, was proof of his lust.

Kuval unbuttoned his pants and pulled out that thick snake. *Fürr*, that thing had been inside me? How was that even possible?

"Open."

My jaw went as wide as it could go, and I wasn't sure if my lips could get around his girth.

"Stick out your tongue."

I did as asked. He slapped his cock on the bed of my out-stretched tongue. Twice. Then he rammed himself inside my mouth. I gagged. His hand kept me in place. But as my throat softened, I could breathe. Kuval remained still letting me get used to his hardness. Soon enough, I suckled his shaft as he'd shown me, and with a moan, Kuval pulled out and then in with a tempo that made me struggle to breathe once again. I gasped air. *Oh, fúrr.* This was hitting my core and pushing every desire button.

Soon we had a rhythm. If my hands weren't behind me, I'd stroke myself to completion. It was erotic. It was everything I'd never ask for. Never admit I wanted. But my moans of delight conveyed the truth. This was turning me on.

I opened my eyes. Kuval tilted his head down, allowing me to see his slack mouth, his hips pumping and his eye-brows lifted high. He was lost in me. I had power over him. Yes. . . this. . . oh, this. . .

Our eyes connected. Not as though we looked at each other so much as into each other. Fúrr blazed in a wild at-tempt to burn him from a glance, but Kuval never looked away. That's when I heard a word in my head. *Ascensorem.*

What it meant I didn't know. But I felt the word to the tail end of my being. He was life. He was death. He was mine. He was the word at the tip of my tongue that I couldn't remember. Everything mattered because Kuval was—

Movement caught the corner of my eye. Five men stalked the alleyway towards us. Through Kuval's jabbing thighs, I recognized the leader strolling in front.

Bemus. Guild master's first lieutenant. The face in place of Arkenu. Wonderful. The humiliation Kuval said he'd shield me from. . . well, I guess even the mighty Kuval couldn't protect me from everything.

I struggled, but Kuval wiped at my cheeks. "Don't. . . I've waited for this. I don't want to stop."

Bemus stood twenty feet away, smirking at me with smug satisfaction. "I now see how you became the Kenwald mascot."

Bemus's men laughed.

Piss off. My ears burned. If I could, I would clench my jaw and stop, except. . . I'd promised. No hurting.

"Ignore him, baby." Kuval never let up, swinging his hips as if we were alone. "Bemus, if you disturb us right now, I *will* kill you."

"Oh, no, please continue." Bemus waved his hand in a flourish. "I like seeing the pet be put in his place."

I growled.

Kuval hissed.

Oh, *furr.* I widened my eyes and looked up. Did I hurt him?

A smile and appreciative gaze met my silent question. "It's fine, baby."

"What the ever-loving elements, Zeroh?" one of Bemus's men said. "If that's how you interrogate a mark, I want to be next."

They all laughed.

My cheeks heated.

"Hey. Don't look at them. They aren't here." Kuval pumped. His eyes soft, tender. Vastly opposite from his cock that he continued to stuff inside my mouth.

But this wasn't what I wanted. To be ridiculed for something that was sacred. It was obvious Kuval took oral sex as something only lovers did. In fact, I didn't get the sense he was a one-off type of guy. Now that I'd gotten to know him, he seemed more of a romantic.

Yes, I had been trying to kill him, but so much happened between us. He wasn't doing this to display me for show or ridicule and laughs at my expense.

Kuval threw an angry look at Bemus. "Get the hell out of here." All the while, his pumping never stopped.

"I'm afraid I have to retrieve the mutt." Bemus laughed.

"Over my dead body."

One of the men started for us. Bemus caught him. "No. This is too amusing."

Great. When this was done, Bemus would muse to everyone about the thief of a rival guild fucking me in the mouth. The lieutenant would say he saved me. Bemus would definitely add other embellishments to his story.

"Screw that." Another man stepped out and threw a five-pointed star at Kuval's back.

Before I could even warn him, Kuval twisted sideways, his cock making a loud pop as he pulled away. He dodged the weapon leaving it stuck in the wall where his chest had been and threw something so fast I couldn't see them until the five small dart-like knives met their mark.

One went to the throat of the guy who attacked first. One went in a subordinate's knee. One found a guy's stomach. Another one stuck out of the fourth's chest, dead center. The last, Bemus caught on his forearm.

Screams erupted. One guy was dead. Kuval somersaulted and planted a foot on the knife implanted in the guy's stomach. Blood spurted. Before a drop of the red spray could land on Kuval, he was already off and moving. He lunged and swiped a fist across a throat. There must have been a knife in Kuval's hand because a crimson line ran along the neck of knifed-in-the-knee guy. Kuval was gone before the man lifted a hand to his wound. Technically, the knee-knifed guy was already dead.

A blade shot out of Kuval's hand. This time it met its true mark in the heart of the last of Bemus's men. He stared at the dagger in his chest, then fell over. Dead.

Kuval landed on his feet. Bemus's eyes glazed over. A glimmer of silver flashed just outside his ear. It was the unfinished handle of Kuval's dart-knife. The lieutenant fell flat on his face. I doubted he was alive when he hit.

A cold burn washed over my veins. Kuval was untouched. He wasn't even breathing hard. Holy *fúrr*. He had been so fast. His accuracy with knives was impressive. Five at once. One I hadn't even seen fly. Two in opposite directions, both hitting their mark perfectly.

"Damn." Kuval rose and looked around. "That took too many tries."

I'd seen death. Been the cause of it. Heard the screams of agony. Even fought with some of the contracts. But I'd never seen anything like this. I'd been witness to the fifth element in action.

"I knew them," I whispered.

Bemus and I had no love for each other, but I hadn't thought of killing him.

Kuval stiffened and shoved himself back in his pants as he walked over to me.

I wasn't sure what to think. Run? Burn? Wait to die? The force of nature squatted down, blocking my view of the five dead Kenwald members.

"When I said you weren't an assassin, this is what I meant." He took hold of my shaking hands and placed soft kisses on my knuckles. Somehow, I'd gotten my hands in front of me during the fight.

My view of him blocked everything else out. "Why did you kill them? They were just going to return me."

His expression hardened. "Like I said. I won't be parted from you. Not by force."

My eyes flew wide. At any time during our first fight, Kuval could have slit my throat, cut my hands off, "off-ed" me at any point.

"Does that frighten you?" His thumbs circled my hands.

Eyebrows raised, I didn't lie. "A little."

He smiled. "Even when you were trying to smoke me, there was no way I could retaliate. You could cinder me to ash and I'd forgive you."

"Not making me feel safer."

He laughed. "Come on. We have to go."

"No one saw us. I can. . . hide them." Or rather give them a proper cremation.

Kuval pulled out one of the vials. "I can douse them with a drop of Fire essence."

"No! I mean. . . if you do that, the Fire won't stop at their bodies." Once *Fúrr* had a hold of fuel, it would do everything to spread and keep going. "Aleenia can't be another Burrow Hills. If you give me permission, I can do it. I won't hurt you." There was no way I could defend against Kuval. He had the upper hand.

His deep-throated laugh echoed off the buildings. "I'm convinced you don't make your marks suffer. But not hurting me and not burning me aren't exactly the same, are they?"

"Now you're being ridiculous." I lifted my manacled hands as proof.

The last of his laughter died, but he smirked in his knowing amusement.

"Why would I burn you? There's this contraption around my neck." I took hold of the pole in between us and shook. The contraption rattled. "If I leave without you someone else will pick up where you left off." I could just imagine myself trying to drag this enchanted necklace with bound hands in the streets. Plenty would attempt to recapture me before I got to Arkenu. The thought of returning to him in this state would do nothing for my reputation.

Kuval remained silent. Waiting. His smile gone, giving me the determined mercenary look. Heat and the unique scent of him washed over me.

"Fine." I rolled my eyes. "I will not burn you. But let me be straight, Kuval, if I get free, all my promises are void."

Sighing, Kuval nodded his head. "I'd expect nothing less." He lifted his chin to the bodies. "It'll give us time. If no one finds this mess, it would be better. No one will miss Bemus for a while." He stood, returning the vial to his belt pouch, looking up at the apartment windows. He pulled the opposite side of the pole-manacle from the wall. "Get up."

I obeyed.

He turned the contraption's handle, and it clicked. The neck swiveled as he walked around me until I was in the lead with the dead men before me and Kuval behind me.

"Okay, Sparky, light 'em up."

I checked with *Fúrr*. My Fire seemed okay with this amendment to our agreement.

Gathering my lust, hate, envy, and most definitely my embarrassment, I closed my eyes concentrating on the bodies before me.

The swirling of *Fúrr* inside me grew to a point rivaling the contents in Kuval's vials. But it wasn't enough. There were five bodies to ash. I'd done this to a handful of marks. Ones in which my sorrow for them boiled to rage. Instantaneous combustion took effort. The targets I'd done this to had felt a bit of heat but had not felt discomfort. I doubted they knew what happened before they died. Even during. But I hadn't tried flaming five people at once.

White Fire could do it. How had I reached that source again?

Damn. Kuval was waiting for me. If he grew impatient, he didn't show it. The need to impress him was a type of pride that had everything to do with courting a mate. I shoved the thought down to *fúrr*, hoping it would burn out like the angst I also threw to feed Fire.

My mind wandered to the man who kept me captive. Lover. Protector. Assassin. *Ascensorem.*

Tingles spread like a wave over my body.

His tentative touches matched his rough handling. I pulled those thoughts out of Fire's hungry fingers. I'd never set my sights strictly on men, but Kuval had shown me *things*. I couldn't name these boundless possibilities. Yearnings started pouring into *fúrr*. I let them. I didn't want to want anyone. Yearnings led to frustration that led to desperation that burned lives, homes, cities. Desire was dangerous.

My Fire started to disintegrate every last emotion before I could feel it. I forced *Fúrr* over to the five bodies.

A whoosh of energy. The smell of burnt flesh. My exhaustion left me leaning against my metal necklace.

Before me the five bodies were gone. Black smudges the only trace of them left.

Kuval whistled. "Impressive."

My legs gave out. Hard dirt bit into my knees.

"Zeroh!" Kuval was at my back, hauling me up.

"I'm okay. Just tired." Feeding everything I had to *Fúrr* wiped me out. "Let me catch my breath."

"If I let you go, will you run?" Kuval whispered in my ear.

"No." I pointed to the black marks on the ground. "I'll turn you to ash."

He chuckled. "Well, unless I'm wrong, a sassy little youth like you won't have much Fire to burn right now."

The metal clamp snapped open, and before I knew it, Kuval lifted me in his arms and carried me out of the alley as if my weight were as inconsequential as a little girl's.

"Kuval. . ."

"I've got you."

Dignity nowhere to be found, I relaxed into his hold. I closed my eyes, pushed out the curious onlookers walking the street, and melted into his strong arms. At least, this way I wouldn't see the horror, the fear in people's eyes.

Other senses compensated for my lack of sight. Kuval's musk. Footsteps. The intimate cradle of arms. I dared to brush my nose against his bare chest. His skin warm, smooth, arousing. My lips curled into a smile from my introspection of how quickly lust rushed to fill the void. After *Fúrr* consumed my emotions as fuel, I was left numb. Empty. Hollow. Uncaring. It was the perfect time for desire to invade my weakened will. Lust was the strongest desire. Hunger a distant second. All else was lost to my thickening cock.

I opened my eyes, yearning to place my growing avidity on someone. But not just anyone. Kuval's intense focus lay on the road ahead. His eyes scanned. His legs stretched in a full-length stride. His grip on me tightening.

"Are we being followed?"

"No." He looked down.

His urgency to get back was explained by the radiating heat in his eyes. The kind of passion that turned into a lover's tryst. I was not the only lascivious one. Heat spread across my face.

Finally, we got through the tower door. My hands still in cuffs, Kuval managed to get us in while holding me.

Our eyes held each other in a grip tighter than steel. Neither of us moved. Neither of us blinked. I dare say neither of us breathed. Then a slow skulk of a smile turned Kuval's face into his usual domineering self.

"You haven't completed your half of the bargain." His voice wrapped around my cock and teased.

The ache begged me to do something. "I always keep my promises."

"Well, you haven't 'guzzled my cum,' yet." He carried me across the room.

"Do you always insist on being so crude?"

"Your words, not mine." Then his lips were against me.

He laid me on the altar that had been my bed for the past week. But he didn't lock my wrists and ankles to the stone. He had other ideas.

Kuval positioned me so that my back was on the cool, flat surface, but my head and neck hung free over the side. Then he unleashed his bulging cock and set his thickness over my lips. Hands tied in front of me, head free, and desire coursing through my veins, I took him down my throat. My own cock hard as the stone table at my back.

There was no more denying this. I wanted him. I wanted the pleasure he gave. I wanted a lover. To feel safe. To let go. To take and to have. I wanted it all.

Kuval leaned over, shoved himself in further down my throat, and took my hardening snake between his lips. The whimper of grateful ecstasy and the shudder of overloading senses were muffled by my full mouth.

Hands pinned me down.

Let go. Kuval's mantra rang in my ears.

He arched his back, letting my cock roll over his lips, thighs pumping. "Zeroh. . ." His voice was a growl.

I smiled in satisfaction. This time he was getting off, and it was entirely my will to make him beg for more.

The rhythm of his hips became faster. I couldn't see his face, but the rumbling of his words urged me on. I curled my tongue around his shaft and sucked until my jaw ached.

"Oh, fuck. . ." Kuval clasped onto my waist and stilled. Manly grunts accompanied surges of spunk shooting too far down my throat to taste. My cock strained as Kuval cried out the last of his orgasm.

He hung his head and panted. Slowly and truly, I grasped that his cock was in my mouth, not just the tip—all of his cock, and what it meant. I wanted this. A part of me would always be his.

Kuval slipped from my mouth and hauled me in a sitting position. My numb hands tingled in relief. They were beginning to become uncomfortable after being bound.

"Zeroh. . ." Kuval whispered. He unbuttoned my pants and swept my coat to the side. How his cock was still hard, I didn't know. His stamina proved more resilient than my own Fire. "I'm going to make love to you."

Shit. His candid words burned my face.

"I'm going to give you the pain you need to forgive yourself," he whispered. "And then I'm going to give you the love you crave."

My hands were between his chest. I could have pushed him away, but didn't. I let him lift me up. He aligned that hot, hard cock of his with my hole and eased me down, impaling me on his length. I breathed in a sharp breath. His girth spread my cheeks to the point I thought I'd get the wind kicked out of me.

"You'll feel my touch until my hands burn into your heart." Kuval nestled his rod all the way inside my ass. "I'll drive out those memories. I'll never let you think yourself unworthy again."

"Unworthy of what? You?" I snarled at the painful memory that was becoming a dull ache.

"Of anything." He turned my head and clasped his lips to mine. His tongue sealed his words as if we were shaking hands on a promise. His will was the sea washing over me. Instead of extinguishing my Fire, his words stoked my ego, raised my confidence, and helped me accept his body inside me. I relaxed, just a little.

Kuval took a mile.

Pain struck upward. Fuck. My ass.

"Breathe." His lips pinned my ear.

I obeyed.

"Good boy."

The tension I'd been holding unfurled. A mesh of want and need collided at the intersection of punishing pain and satisfying pleasure. The war of the past clawed at me to remember my guilty mistake. But my memories faded as the present task master punished me, aroused me, took my regret, and helped me serve my sentence.

"Stick with me, and I'll make sure you pay for your mistake, enough to set you free."

Strange how Kuval was setting my conscience to rights. But I didn't need to tell the man. His ego was already bigger than his reputation. But that confidence was also what set me at ease.

His hands helped me along to the final culmination. Before I could warn him of my impending orgasm, he placed a vial over the tip of my cock.

There was something different about this newly purchased container, but I didn't ponder on the difference. I rocked with the motion and let my release out as if my cum were not a destructive force ready to burn the world. The relief was immeasurable. I melted into Kuval's body. Bliss spread warmth through my limbs. I floated in ecstasy. In peace. It was like coming home to find Burrow Hills whole and unscathed.

Kuval took the vial off my tip and corked the top. "Interesting, it's white."

There, swirling in glass, sparkled white liquid. It was different from all the other times I'd cum into a bottle. Not only was the color different, but this batch seemed more—dangerous.

The tiniest sound of cracking glass shot panic through me. "Kuval..."

Before I could move, the tube shattered.

CHAPTER 14

ZEROH

GLASS SHARDS FLEW. HORROR slowed my response. Fire spread up the walls, claiming the long table. Before I could blink, white Fire climbed up the stone walls and blanketed the wood ceiling. A sea of flame rippled like waves over the wood.

I brought my chained wrists up where I could use my hands to—what? Orchestrate the destruction?

A box was shoved into my hands. Kuval lifted me onto his shoulder about as kindly as a duffle bag.

Fire raged around us and turned inward, towards the oxygen. Towards us. The heat was so intense it curled my eyelashes. Kuval ran out the back door with only me, the box of vials in my hands, and his metal contraption. His feet pounded the ground.

Fire claimed the water tower. Flames threw themselves skyward. The entire structure was engulfed. It happened too fast for my brain to follow after the sweetness of Kuval sending me to ecstasy.

Water rushed out the back door like a narrowly held back ocean. Kuval's jarring strides hit against my hips. We weren't going to make it. The screams of Hydra reached my ears. Mad, furious screeches of Water chased after its assailant. Me.

A ripple of fear tickled down my spine.

How stupid could I be? This was always the end result. Destruction. That's all I was. For a fleeting moment, I'd thought I could have something other than shame. I was the fool. Never again. Certainly never if Kuval didn't have a plan to scale the wall.

Water tumbled towards us fast as horse hooves. Hydra had a mind to trample me under its liquid weight. In its attempt to burn me before taking us over, the rapids threw foamy drops at me. Water dotted my sleeves. The top of my hands stung from tiny spherical projectiles.

I heard the click-clank of the metal rod, and then we were soaring. Kuval swung us up to a thick tree branch and sat me against the main trunk. He'd lifted us out of the torrent.

As he stared down, at the outer wall below, I followed his gaze right where I'd left a huge, gaping hole in the wall.

Water crashed into the barrier. White foam rose and curled back in on the flow. But a few more bricks tumbled. The force of Water when it wanted out was patient and unstoppable. And Water wanted through the wall.

The hole was large enough that a stream poured out onto the other side and helped crumble the stone. The walls demise seemed probable. The stream making its way through a funnel escaped out the enclosure to the city beyond. At least, it was headed towards the sea and not into downtown.

"Damn!" Kuval raked a hand through his hair.

So, he does get flustered. I needed to stop thinking about him as a man. He was my mark. But there was no denying he saved my life. I set down the box of vials and focused on the metal clamps around my wrists. I poured every memory of all that happened during the week into my *Fúrr*. Focusing on the metal, I poured my Fire into burning off my restraints.

Within minutes, the steel melted off. The slag plopped into hissing Water.

I stood and as I balanced on the branch, exhausted. My pants slipped down to my knees. I'd forgotten they needed buttoning and shuffled my clothes to rights. Of course, Kuval already had himself tucked away, leaving me with my dick out.

The thief concentrated on the flow of Water now creating a river. The water tower that was set ablaze tumbled, but *Fúrr* still raged despite floating in soaked wood. White Fire danced on top of the flowing Water. As if the rapids were fuel. Hydra hissed, popped, screamed, and tossed white foam clawing to get away from its nemesis.

Steam billowed. Water boiled. All the while White Fire laughed in crackles and snaps. Tormenting its foe like a fly landing stinging bites over and over on exposed skin.

"This isn't good." Kuval shifted and looked back at me. "There are only three towers for the whole city."

I straightened to my full height and glowered back. "What do I care?"

He did a double take then stood and faced me. "Don't."

"Don't what?" I snarled. "Don't kill you now that I'm free?"

He leveled me with a measured stare. "Don't pretend this means nothing." He waved between us. "Don't pretend what we have means nothing."

My heart hurt. But we couldn't be together. It would end in ash.

"What do you know?" I flicked my hand in dismissal. "As an expert in Pyromages, you should know *Fúrr* eats its host from the inside out. I throw every emotion I have to keep my Fire alive. I am the uncaring monster everyone thinks I am." My eyes stung. My heart throbbed. For once in my life I needed to do the right thing. Wish I knew what the right thing was.

More bricks fell into a now steady gush of Water.

"I know it takes a lot more than fleeting one-nighters for a Pyragon to burn through metal." He pointed at my wrists. "Still going to tell me we mean nothing?"

The top of the wall tumbled. Water tumbled over the "V" pathway. The stream became a vandfald. A waterfall.

"Screw you."

"So soon?" He smiled.

I scowled, upturned my palm, and let a fist sized flame linger in my hand. "I owe you, for saving my life."

"At least twice. Likely three times." His smirk goaded me well enough, but I didn't take the bait.

"For that, I'll let you go. But the next time we meet, don't expect such leniency." Thank *fúrr*, my voice remained steady. I'd forever avoid him at all costs. The thought weighed my heart. A bar of gold was lighter than the shattering lump in my chest. He'd opened a door inside me. But like all the other places, chaos ensued wherever I prolonged my welcome.

"So, this is it, huh?" Kuval smirked. "You think this is the last time we'll see each other?"

"You're still my mark. I wouldn't advise another meeting." My fireball grew. But I was using the same endless energy that felt more like affection than hate.

"Well then, I look forward to next time." Kuval grabbed the box of vials in a sweeping arm. "But for now, there's something I need to take care of."

With the metal contraption wrapped around the tree branch, Kuval swung over the river. Water corroded the wall enough to pour forth like a river. He released the clamp and landed with nimble grace on the flat top side of a wood barrel.

I snorted. He'd taken off before I could distract him with a fireball. My plan *had been* to throw him off guard to escape. Guess that wasn't necessary.

Kuval rode the waves, his silhouette a surf rider conquering the new canal flowing southbound, towards the ocean. And with him my heart. Everything ached. Especially my eyes watching him go. Despair cloaked the memories running through my mind. Despite his threat, I would never see him again and the thought put a lump in my throat. I watched his silhouette until he was out of sight. All the while my heart skipped calling out for him.

Fúrr. I've ruined everything.

The Fire cultivating in my palm extinguished. Water flowed in a torrent beneath me. Great. How was I supposed to get out of here?

Measuring the distance from the tree branch to the unbroken part of the wall, I used Wind to make sure I leaped

far enough away from the compromised top. The water
tower was far enough away from town that people hadn't
gathered yet. I climbed down, concealing myself behind
the stone and snuck away avoiding any accusatory fingers.
They'd be right in that I burned down a third of their water
supply. I deserved to go to Brogan and not as the safe haven
Arkenu housed me in for the past few months.

Concealing myself with the lapels of my coat and casting
my eyes downward, I traveled the dirty lanes of Aleenia.
I'd heard it was once a place of great wealth and knowledge. Even in antiquity, there were telltale marks of that
truth if you looked at details. A proper cleaning across the
doorways would show permanent address markings that
stood the test of time. Under peeled paint, frescoes peeked
out from the newer layer meant to cover the art. And the
fact that thousand-year-old buildings still stood, though
crumbling, gave precedence to long-dead genius architects.
Yes, the city was aging. But it was the oldest city in recorded
history. It was time to leave before I brought the whole
place down.

My book. Damn. That tome managed to survive Fire.
Maybe, I could go back and see if it survived Water. No.
It was only a matter of time before someone spotted me
shifting through mud and figured out what happened. I
burned a quarter of the city's water supply. They'd come
for me. The penalty for starting a never-ending Fire was
death.

I passed into a deserted alleyway and set my head against
the oak door of the secret passageway to Brogan.

But Brogan wasn't even an option for me. Arkenu
was good, but he wasn't preventing-people-from-lynch-
ing-me-after-that-spectacle good. Dozens of Hydromages

must be on their way to quench what I'd started. People would know Arkenu's Pyromage would be involved in this.

This door was my crossroads. If I opened it, I would have to face my guild master and explain why Bemus was dead, why the city lacked a third of its water supply, and my betrayal of his command not to go after Kuval. If I turned and walked out of the city, I'd be on the run with no allies and no food.

As I leaned against the door of decision a black shadow crept up from my boots to the very hairs on my head.

Fate had never been kind to me.

Reluctantly, I stepped away from the oak door and turned. There, shielding the alley's exit was the imposing, cloaked form of the very person I hadn't wanted to disappoint most. *Hadn't.* Past tense.

"Arkenu! Guild Master." I gasped at his dark eyes filled with disappointment. The similarity of Arkenu's and Kuval's faces rattled me. All of my air was stolen by the thought of Kuval, not my guild master, looking at me in discontent. My knees buckled. It was a near thing I didn't go down. If Kuval had looked at me during our parting as Arkenu did now, I would have begged for mercy. Done anything Kuval wanted. Even gone with him.

"Zeroh," Arkenu, my guild master, glided to me. His six-foot-two frame menaced over me, and his larger-than-life shadow blotted out the sun. "Come. I need you."

Not the end!
There will be more of the Pyromage series
Book 2 coming soon

THANK YOU

THANK YOU, MY VERY kind beta readers who have all helped me get this far. But a huge thank-you needs to go out to Monica, Lea, and Crystal. Thank you for believing in me. And thank you for making the book stronger by your thoughts. Great appreciation, always.

ABOUT S.N. MCKIBBEN

Will Write For Puppy Chow!

Slave to a playful pack of five dogs and her notoriously sluggish computer affectionately known as "Dave", Stephanie crafts Dirty Stories featuring Underdog Heroes revolving around Social Taboos. When she's not writing, you can catch her wandering between the trees of her twenty-seven-acre property in Central Texas that she shares with her partner and their furry companions. Her life has all the elements of a graphic novel—sometimes twisted, sometimes funny, but always beautiful and its title is Adventure. Come play!

ALSO BY S.N. MCKIBBEN

Join the fun with Author S.N. McKibben for give-aways, updates and new release opportunities at:
https://www.snmckibben.com/
Other books by S.N. McKibben:

Notice Me Senpai series

Seducing Sensei
Redeeming Senpai

Enemies to Lovers

The Silent Road
A Blind Curve

Pyromage series

To Tame a Dragon

<u>**Standalones**</u>

Lady Alene and the Widower
But For You, Yes
Cougar Bait in the Coffee Shop
The Demon Inside Me
Escape to Vampire Dam
Spoils of Allsveil
Dr. Vampyre

www.ingramcontent.com/pod-product-compliance
Lightning Source LLC
Chambersburg PA
CBHW022145240626
47153CB00007B/2518